WILDERNESS SPA

ALSO BY JIM HALVERSON

Ponce: What Actually Happened at the Fountain of Youth

Trials and Trails: Adventures and Unexpected Discoveries of Life

Wilderness
SPA

WHERE PHYSICAL SURVIVAL
MEETS PSYCHOLOGICAL SURVIVAL

JIM HALVERSON

Gail Force Publishing

Dedicated to:

A Level Playing Field

CHAPTER 1

September 27, 1:20 PM

Tom scanned the forest clearing. He'd hiked five miles up a trail padded with evergreen needles and moss to a small creek that flowed out of the modest mountains. A low overcast coated the day, and wisps of moisture circulated gently among the trees. Silence permeated everything, which caused Tom to carefully avoid scuffing the soil with his boot or breaking a twig on the ground. Not that a little noise would disturb anything other than the momentary silence, but it was a kind of game Tom played with himself at such times. Particularly, the game honed skills he depended upon.

The hills and low mountains surrounded the area where his family lived on a small homestead. Tom's father had built a substantial log cabin between a small idyllic meadow and the main river, deep in the Alaskan interior wilderness. The meadow now grew vegetables and responded to meticulous work by his mother. Long before Tom was born, Tom's father had discovered dependable amounts of gold in the stream Tom now tended. Tom and his father operated a sluice box on the stream that still delivered consistent small amounts of gold dust. The gold they had extracted to date made decent wages, but like all prospectors, they were aware the stream could lead to a major lode, though Tom's family wasn't dependent on more gold. They were content with their life in the wilderness; if a notable increase in gold entered their lives, little would change.

Every step Tom took was purposefully considered for reasons more important than maintaining the pristine silence. For the moment, this small clearing belonged to him. The wisps of moisture, the trees that grew into the mist, the gurgling small stream, and the silence fit Tom perfectly. The arctic afforded infinite attractions, depending upon your point of view. Scenery, serenity, landscapes, fresh air, wildlife, and danger all offered opportunities and challenges.

Danger was always on Tom's mind. A lot of things in this wilderness could hurt you. Enough of them had caused Tom discomfort to make him aware of his surroundings. He didn't spend a lot of time considering the benefits independently or as something other than an integral part of his life. He worked in and around the scenery and the landscapes. Serenity happened when he fell asleep. He breathed the fresh air, and he ate and wore the wildlife. Danger, he couldn't disregard. He didn't just survive; he lived in the wilderness. He was good at it, and he didn't mind the work. He thrived on it. In the homestead, he had other interests beyond survival, but out here, anywhere beyond the homestead confines, he paid attention. He paid attention, but his focus wasn't fear based; it was simply his way of living in the present.

Despite his relatively young age of twenty-two, he qualified uniquely to function in his arctic home. Physically, he presented a superb specimen: five feet ten inches tall, one-hundred-ninety pounds, and all muscle. His father had raised him in the wilderness and passed on all the skills he had accumulated. Along with the white-man's skills and tools his father passed on to him, his mother, a full-blooded Alaskan Indian, carefully taught him native skills and attitudes. In addition to his home schooling, Tom's father decided that his son should also be exposed to some lower-forty-eight civilization. From the age of five, Tom and his family spent the hardest part of the arctic winter in Fort Yukon, where Tom then attended school in town. He enjoyed those days in school, and even now, he often considered them. He had a unique ability to meld lessons from school into the wilderness and survival.

Tom's father, John, had come to the arctic after applying his education in the corporate world for a few years. He could have stayed, worked the rat race, and lived comfortably in the suburbs. But something about the wilds of Alaska called him. John, single, healthy, and looking for adventure, sold everything. He traded his convertible automobile for an old pickup truck and drove to Alaska. He took a job in a small interior town, saved some money, learned about the wilderness, and finally set off on his own. John learned about the wilderness by spending all his free time in it. Friends in town talked with him freely about what he had seen. By helping his friends, John learned how to build cabins, boats, and traps; how to hunt and fish; and how to be independent. When he was ready, he set off for the wilderness.

He never looked back from his homestead. John ensured that he and his family kept up with the rest of the world during the winters in Fort Yukon. He was adamant that Tom would eventually have a choice of how he would spend his life. Choices were always important.

Aside from the winters in town, Tom and his family maintained an interesting library at the homestead. Tom not only read all the books, but he studied them and often instigated family debates over controversial passages. Tom's intellectual curiosity pleased his parents.

Eventually, they knew it was time to pause the annual passages and give Tom an opportunity to discover the rest of the world. John intended to present the plan to Tom within a few weeks on their semiannual trip down the river. Tom's mother would miss him, but she also knew he had outgrown the life they were able to afford him in the wilderness. And she, like John, wanted their son to have options.

Tom commanded his way in the wilderness. At the homestead, intellectual pursuits kept his mind active. He thought the day would come when he would spend some time in the lower forty-eight, but for now, he had everything he needed.

Tom rested his rifle on a tree after checking the area and walked to the thirty-foot-long gold-mining sluice. He had built the sluice by hollowing out a tree trunk and carving ridges to catch the heaviest materials as the rushing water washed away lighter worthless black sand and gravel. He carefully dusted the black sand off the catch ridges and used a syringe to collect gold dust from each catch area. In the last catch area, he found a pea-sized nugget, the largest piece of gold he had found in this part of the stream. That discovery encouraged him to think that as he moved up the stream, he would continue to find more and larger nuggets. He shoveled sand and gravel from around the ancient creek bed into the sluice that allowed the natural forces to work their magic. He figured he would have to move the sluice upstream next season. For now, he filled the sluice by carrying the sand and gravel a shovelful at a time from undisturbed soil near the active streambed to the sluice. In all, he figured he had retrieved about five hundred dollars of gold for the week's collection. Not bad, he thought. It would help the family get through the winter in town. Tom and his family would take their boat down the river for the winter within a few weeks.

After collecting the gold dust and depositing it in a leather pouch, Tom walked across the small clearing and climbed a crumbly hillside toward a rocky peak that he had climbed a few times over the years. He scaled the steep solitary peak a rock at a time. He wanted a view of the upper main river valley for game and water conditions. He leaned his rifle on a boulder and sat next to the ledge. Straight down, he looked at the tops of trees. Looking out, Tom watched the river as it wound its way through miles of brush, gravel banks, and swampy areas. In the far distance, the river exited high canyon walls carved from even taller mountains. Far on the other side of the mountains, the north-slope tundra extended further than Tom had ever ventured. He and his father had explored the mountains all the way to the tundra two years earlier. Tom thought about that trip and wondered what they would have found if they had continued. He had read about the tundra, and that slice of knowledge gave him a curious desire to experience life on the tundra: no borders, and wolves, geese, ducks, swans, and magnificent caribou herds. All that wildlife and more subsisted here in his home, but on the tundra, it came in unlimited waves.

After a few peaceful minutes and timeless memories, the entire mountain shook—in fact, all the land shook violently, and continued to shake. The devastating jolts dislodged Tom from the rock he had claimed. He rolled over and scrambled to secure his hold on that stable rock. His legs hung over the ledge as he fought for his life to reclaim his hold. Finally, a good grip and strength allowed him to pull himself back onto the ledge. He crawled back, away from the edge. When the shaking subsided momentarily, he realized that his rifle was lost over the narrow ledge and buried by the landslide of boulders two hundred feet below. He consolidated his position on the peak, waited, and observed. What he saw, astonished him. The river shriveled and then swelled again. The water flow undulated indifferently while he watched. Rumblings from rockslides echoed down the river. Trees swayed, mountains shook, and the river shivered as Tom clung to his perch.

When nature's powers calmed, he scrambled down the mountainside as intermittent rumblings continued. Tom backed away from the peak and watched loose material find new resting places. He walked toward his sluice and noted that it was only slightly dislocated but still intact, with water washing his latest shovel-loads of gravel. Without his rifle, Tom studied the area one last time and started down the trail. As often happened, the low mist turned to light rain. He frequently ran down this trail. Today, intermittent rumblings, rain, and general uncertainty forced Tom to move slowly and carefully. He'd never experienced an earthquake anything like this. The way the river heaved, rushed, and shriveled could change the family's float to Fort Yukon.

Halfway down the path, he thought that it was strange for his father's trash fire to put off that much smoke. He continued anxiously down toward the homestead. Before Tom rounded the final hillock, the final approach to home, he was horrified to see the sky filled with heavy, dark smoke. Now he had to run. He was breathless when he reached the homestead.

Nothing was left except smoldering timbers and a few flickering flames. He called out. No answer. He called again and looked around the homestead perimeter, into the trees. Then up and down the river. Nothing. He noticed the dogs weren't even barking. He walked through wet debris into an attached dog yard and found his dogs burned to death. He focused on the cabin, or the ashes that had been the cabin, and found his parents' remains under the charred roof timbers. The timbers had crushed them when the roof collapsed. The earthquake and fire destroyed everything, even the family boat in the attached shed that was still engulfed by twisting flames. That boat would have carried the family to Fort Yukon for the winter.

Tom continued walking through the cinders. He tried to focus on little things. He investigated where his bedroom had been. Nothing. Everything was reduced to ashes. Even his books, *Philosophers of the World, Geology, Great Essays, Poems by Robert Service, Short Stories by Jack London*; all gone. The kitchen, where his mother had always made things civilized: burned, crumpled, and destroyed.

In a matter of mere minutes, his life went from having a secure family, pets, personal enlightenment escapes, and his clothes— to nothing, not even a gun.

Tom found a waterproof tarp and wrapped himself in it as he leaned against the old tall tree in the yard. It was one of the trees his father would never touch. He said it was the grandfather in the grove. Tom couldn't believe it. He just couldn't believe it. The scene, and the whole situation, drove home the adage that he had always believed: "You can do everything right, and still be wrong."

Tom wasn't concerned for his own existence. That thought never entered his mind. He'd endured the wilderness before. But he was sick to his stomach and probably didn't care if he survived. He closed his eyes, not able to look at the reality that faced him. He pulled the tarp over his head and slept, almost as though unconscious, through the night.

When he opened his eyes, nothing had changed. The disaster still faced him. He worked on the only thing he could do. He found a shovel and dug a grave. Then he shoveled his parents' ashes into the pit. The task would have been monumental for most people. Tom had often faced the reality of life and death in the arctic, but he had never considered the possibility of burying his parents. Now, he just did it. Tom shoveled a small mound over the site, placed a ring of stones around it, and contemplated what they had meant to him. It was almost everything.

Tom walked slowly around the homestead several times, remembering good times and hard times, but times always filled with companionship and good will. The ashes remaining in the pile from which he had shoveled his parents held his attention. It was the hand-hewn beam his father had proudly told him about. How he felled the tree, carved the beam, and levered it into place by himself. One of the feats that demonstrated his father's ingenuity and independence. That was behind him. Tom's only concern now was to leave, the homestead, the memories. He had to get away.

He went to the detached cellar and considered his immediate needs for the trip down the river. One item, certainly not a survival necessity on the trip but valuable for the winter, was the family's accumulated gold. He estimated the stash weighed almost two pounds. At that point, Tom had no intention of returning to the homestead. He didn't want to burden himself with a worthless two pounds on the trail, but he would need it to get through the winter. He tied the pouch in the bottom of his pack, then filled the rest of his backpack with flour, potatoes, onions, bear fat, dried meat, salt, and sugar.

Then, for the last time, he surveyed what had been the family home. He knew what he had to do. Stay Alive. Tom's life in the wilderness had prepared him for just another trek down the river. He would follow his small river until it entered the next picturesque river. One that afforded rafters the opportunity to experience the wilderness during the summer. Then he would make his way down that river to the confluence of the Porcupine River. After a short time on the Porcupine, he would find the Yukon River, then up the river to Fort Yukon. He knew the route. It wouldn't be fun, but fun wasn't something he craved. Just face the tasks at hand, he told himself.

Dressed in leather pants and shirt, an oilskin knee-length coat, lace-up rubber boots, and a waterproof brimmed hat, Tom started toward the river. He wished he had his gun, but he didn't dwell on it. A long knife hung from his belt; he would travel light and fast.

He knew there were fish in the river and that was good and bad. He would have fish to eat, but he knew the bears would also be fishing. Tom's father had picked this part of the river for his homestead for all good reasons. Regular salmon runs, moose, bears, fur bearers, and majestic landscapes. The wide canyon guided the river through neatly sloped gravel banks that ran up to the base of steep mountains or opened onto lush meadows. All the mountainsides supported opulent timber with a thick understory. Conditions would change, but for now, Tom put one foot in front of the other.

Just before dark, he used his nylon cord to hoist his pack up a tree for safety. He chewed on some jerky as he walked to the riverbank. He scanned the river up and down and marveled at the debris it had deposited high above the current water level as the river had heaved and churned during the earthquake. After surveying the area, Tom hiked up the hill a hundred feet, hollowed out a space in the soft ground and leaves, and rolled himself in his tarp. He tried to sleep. He couldn't. The reality of his parents' death wouldn't allow it. What if he hadn't gone up the trail? What if they'd been digging in the garden? What if they'd taken the dogs out? "What if" wasn't a phenomenon Tom often dealt with. His life consisted of too much reality to deal in make-believe or wishes. Now, he couldn't help it.

Unlike almost anybody else on the river, he wasn't concerned about his own survival. That concern had no place in his mind. His head ached for how empty his life would be without the only family he had. He knew some names in Fort Yukon. He even remembered some friends he went to school with that still lived in town. For a few moments, he considered Janet and hoped he would have a good reunion with her at the market where she helped her parents. None of those thoughts gave him much comfort. He had never made a commitment to Janet, just a friendship. He visited a fishing village on the coast once, but that was even more remote than Fort Yukon.

One thought that entertained him for a while was the idea of trekking over the mountains and disappearing forever with his mother's people. That plan consumed some energy. After some more thinking, he rejected the notion. He had only a vague concept where her village might be, he had never met any family members, and he had no names. Considering his mother's family sparked his memories of how precious his mother had been. Her garden proved more than her green thumb abilities. She used the garden to teach Tom good nutrition, an endeavor she hoped would direct him away from the perils of alcohol. Alcohol was a blight on her people that she was all too familiar with. After graduating from the University of Alaska with a degree in political science, she had taken a job in Fort Yukon as a social worker. That's where she met Tom's father on his way into the wilderness. After Tom's parents married, his mother slowed his father's move into the wilderness because she hoped she could make a difference in the community. After disappointing failures regarding the community's alcohol problems, she gave up and urged John to take her away. During the family stays in Fort Yukon, she continued to volunteer, however.

Those thoughts and others allowed Tom to smile as he considered spending the winter in the family house, now his house, in Fort Yukon. It seemed the most likely scenario. He would make decisions in Fort

Yukon later. Now, his only concern was to get there. He struggled through the night and resumed his trek before the sun came up.

At midday, he walked to the edge of a forested area, a typical landscape where the trees on the steep mountain grew to the edge of the river. From that vantage, he had a view down the river. Three bears were fishing in shallow water where a small stream flowed slowly into the main river. The bears occupied themselves with necessities, and although they might have smelled him, they couldn't distract themselves. Tom knew he would never challenge the bears. He had to work around them. He could cross the river, or he could climb partway up the mountain to go around the bears. He chose to climb the mountain. Two hours later, he returned to the river without incident. Soon he came upon another, smaller stream with no bears. Salmon were working their way up the stream.

Tom removed his pack and waded into the stream. He found the fish's favored channel and positioned his hands. On his second try, he flipped a four-pound salmon onto the beach. He climbed out of the stream, cleaned the fish, and ate the fresh salmon eggs, one of his favorite meals. Then he filleted the fish and stored the precious flesh in a plastic box with a sealed lid. He knew of more fishing areas down the river and never considered taking more than his immediate needs.

He trekked down the river until almost dark, started a small fire, and cooked enough fresh fish for dinner and breakfast. Then he hoisted his pack, leaned against a tree trunk, and inspected the night sky. As he stared into the blank atmosphere, the aurora borealis began to dance for him. That gave him some peace, and he let his mind go blank as he watched the light show. Eventually, clouds covered the sky and Tom went to sleep with a clear head. At daylight, the trek continued in a light rain. Despite his loss and uncertain future, Tom moved down along the river. This was now his reality—living in the present, in real time—the trees, river, mountains, weather, sounds, silence; despite the loss of his parents, Tom was in his environment.

CHAPTER 2

September 27, 1:35 PM

Branch gave the order to the canoes following him to paddle into the still river backwater as they approached one of the first real photo opportunities. They had been paddling through some minor white water and other stretches on the river shrouded in tall dark trees. There had been few places to stop where they were able to do anything other than eat, sleep, and move on. Now they faced an open area brimming with lush fall colors and more. Branch stepped out of the canoe and helped Paul and Sandy onto the beach. Then he secured his canoe with a nylon cord from the canoe to the remnants of a large tree stump on the gravel riverbank before he held Jim's canoe. Jim stepped out and caught Rick's canoe.

With the crews landed on the gravelly beach, the river campers stood in awe of an ice wall climbing out of the still water. They had paddled into a small bay near the base of the glacier. They stared at the glacial face a hundred feet high. The glacier almost came to life. White ice, ancient blue streaks of compressed ice, black and gray trails of soil picked up along its travels over thousands of years were all clues to its ancient existence. When they listened, the campers could even hear it talk to them. Dark groans and creaks welcomed them to an ancient living and dying landscaper.

Branch directed the campers to carry their personal gear high up onto the gravel bank. Jim, Branch, and Rick carried camp supplies up another section of the bank away from the glacier and the bay.

These three oversized canoes were Jim's specialty. Fully loaded, they easily carried all the supplies and equipment the campers would need for a month in the wilderness. The canoes were the most critical equipment, capable of carrying them back to civilization. Branch always inspected each canoe at the end of the day. He also had stowed a repair kit in each canoe in a watertight compartment, and in one canoe he'd packed an emergency radio and a locator, similar to what downed pilots used. Jim always emphasized to his clients that three or four people could safely paddle the canoes down the river if they were willing to follow directions. This trip was advertised as a true arctic adventure, including primary paddling responsibilities. All reservations for this trip required a certification of health and a willingness and ability to paddle.

When most of the packs, bags, supplies, and equipment rested safely on the high gravel bank, Jim advised everybody to prepare for a photo safari before they set up their tents. The campers retrieved their cameras and began arranging and focusing shots of the river, distant snow-coated mountaintops, each other, and the glacier.

Jim gathered the campers around him and offered a tutorial, emphasizing safety on ice and snow. "Alright, let's get up onto that glacier while we've got good light." The group clambered up through the brush and rubble on the bare mountainside toward the glacier. Rocks, from huge boulders to gravel, covered the area. They had been freed from glacial ice after thousands of years in frozen confines.

Jim owned the small Alaska river-camping company. He prided himself on his ability and connections that allowed him to offer his guests good food, good photo opportunities, and safety. He continued to remind the group to keep up; there would be time to take pictures of the flowers later. After a thirty-minute hike, the group spread out on the moraine uphill from the glacial ice to take pictures. Jim knew where the sun would be, and the light was nearly perfect. Gray clouds in the distance provided contrast. But he also knew if they delayed, the clouds could ruin the excellent light and prospects. Given the opportunities, great shots nourished the photographers' enthusiasm.

"Too bad Branch couldn't come up here," Roberta said. Branch, Jim's favorite guide, was in prime physical condition, an expert in wilderness survival, and an excellent cook. Jim liked to take single women on his trips simply because he liked to watch them swoon over Branch. He commanded every aspect of camp life, and Jim never questioned Branch's actions. Branch made the trip secure. Without him, Jim would have re-examined the possibilities of a trip this daring and this late in the year. Weather is always uncertain in this part of the world, but especially once autumn arrived. The permit for this trip didn't come easy. It was initially denied until Jim assured the authorities that Branch would be taking the primary guide responsibilities. Branch's reputation in wilderness survival gave him opportunities denied many other guides. "He's been up here. He's moving the canoes up near the glacier, away from the river, for safety," Jim replied to Roberta.

Jim gathered the group to share his personal history of this glacier. He pointed up the canyon and indicated where the ice had covered the ground over a thousand feet further up the canyon from them less than ten years earlier. A short talk described how glacial streams flowed within the glacier and how at times they surfaced and spewed ice-cold geysers onto the surface. The photo enthusiasts listened to tips about how to get the most out of photographing ice and ice-defined landscapes.

Jim told them that before he turned them loose on the glacier, he wanted a group photo. "Okay, everybody, gather next to the ice for a picture; you'll all get copies of the group photos. I'll climb out onto the edge of the glacier and shoot back across the ice. I want you to have documentation of what has happened to this glacier," Jim said. He cautiously walked out onto what was left of the glacier he had watched shrink significantly over the last several years. Jim reached the edge of the ice, looked down and waved to Branch below him, who had just brought the last empty canoe up close to the base of the glacier, near a safe and open place to secure them.

Without warning, Jim was gone over the edge. The ground and ice shook violently and everyone in the group reduced themselves to hands and knees on the gravel-based moraine. As the ground rumbled, huge fissures developed in the ice. Then with a thunderous roar, most of the ice crumbled and collapsed into the water below. Within seconds, the group was alone on the moraine, overlooking a missing glacier.

Strong rumblings continued for several seconds before any of the campers spoke. "I think we better get back away from this, now," Paul said. Shaken, scared, and uncertain of the severity of the situation, the campers huddled. Before they made their way down to level ground near the river, they watched substantial rubble slide off the mountainside on the opposite canyon wall. Now they were unsure of the river. The water heaved and surged up the banks and then rushed away, carrying away some of Branch's camp equipment. Paul stopped along the way several times to photograph the river's contortions before joining the group.

Once they were back on the riverbank, the campers walked around, attempting to reconcile the proposed campsite with the reality of what remained. Some of the dry bags were scattered from the rock face where they left them. Some of the camp supplies had been carried off by falling ice and floated down the river. The canoes and Branch were gone. Jim had simply disappeared, nowhere to be seen. Before long, the terrifying realization that Jim, Branch, and the canoes were buried under thousands of tons of ice came into focus.

Confusion and a lack of leadership prevailed. Ben and Walt got together and decided to find their tent and supplies. They had left their families at home with the business so they could venture forth into "the rough and tough Alaskan wilderness," as they had described it to their wives. The two men were partners in a wholesale nursery business in Southern California. Ben, a Black man, grew up on a small family farm in Alabama and left for good when he earned a baseball scholarship to UCLA. After graduating with a degree in accounting, he went to work as an accountant in a small firm. Walt's family raised him in their family retail nursery. Walt, a white man, met Ben when Ben hired him to landscape his front yard. Ben was intrigued with how Walt transformed a mess into beauty with flowers and trees. They formed a fast friendship and decided to build a landscaping business together.

They set all their camping equipment and supplies aside next to the rock cliff. When they looked over their fellow river campers, the sight provided little encouragement. The two couples stood alone and hugged their mates. Rick, the lone remaining expedition employee, looked lost as he stared at the ice that confined his employer. He appeared and acted young, about twenty-two, tall, well-muscled, and pleasant. If only he knew anything about survival, the situation would be better.

Ashley wandered down to the water's edge and scanned the river up and down. She was gorgeous, a thirty-year-old computer-network executive from Northern California. Her partner planned to join her on the trip, but her partner's company had entered into a merger agreement and needed her legal expertise without exception. Ashley grew up on a ranch in northern Nevada and knew her way around open country, but she was probably not able to get them out of this situation.

Paul and Sandy had selected this Alaska trip to get away from delicately prepared food served with silver and fine china. They owned and managed a successful high-end restaurant in Cleveland. They thought they could benefit from seeing the other side of food. Regular trips to the gym kept them fit. In their early fifties, they came on the trip looking forward to learning to paddle a canoe. Like many successful couples, they had strong opinions. More importantly, like successful people, they didn't let their opinions destroy opportunities to develop relationships. Paul had brought a good part of his expensive photography equipment on the adventure. He had anticipated some shots of wildlife in their natural environment, without ear tags or brands. He had found ear tags and brands on the wildlife on a recent photo trip to South Dakota, and that aspect ruined the shoot for him. He wanted it natural and untamed.

Jerry and Roberta hailed from Seattle. Jerry worked for a company that supplied, among other things, classified materials to the military. Jerry grew up in the East with a family name that meant something there. He was educated at the best schools. After MIT, he helped develop a guidance system for mobile weaponry. When the company moved to Seattle, he went with them. As an assistant vice president, he lived a comfortable life. Regarding his health, he would say that the doctor said he was five pounds over his normal weight. When asked about his normal weight, he would confess that his normal weight was five pounds overweight. Jerry's friends enjoyed his company. Roberta wrote a political column for Washington papers. She considered it an important hobby when she started. Local demand for more turned her hobby into an obsession. She enjoyed poking barbs at political hypocrisy, had no use for liars, and always pointed out logical fallacies whenever a politician veered off the straight and narrow. Roberta's father was a college basketball coach and she assumed his aggressive methods.

Alaskans would call a group like this "cheechakos," a Chinook Jargon term Robert Service used in his poems about the Yukon to describe newcomers that didn't fit in. On the riverbank with no experienced leader, they felt the part. The light began to fade, and nobody considered standard practices. Tents remained in the dry bags, and there was no fire; nobody had even collected firewood. Finally, Roberta said that even if they didn't eat anything other than trail mix, they should at least set up their tents. That realization triggered some activity. They consolidated the dry bags and sorted out what they would need to get through the night. When the tents stood and they had the gear sorted, they decided to find firewood for the morning fire. With a poor result, they crawled into their tents and worried. They didn't know what to worry about, but they were worried.

In the chilly morning, more reality set in. Nobody had started a fire for them. A light mist added to their frustration. Under normal circumstances, Branch would have constructed a community area under a tarp he had hoisted over a fire and all the camp supplies. In addition to that, he would have had coffee brewed and breakfast started. Rick would have helped him. That's what the campers had paid for.

Ben looked at the campsite and said, "Let's start from scratch. See if you can get some of that wood to burn. I'll search for more." Walt, Paul, and Jerry joined Ben in bringing in more wood. It turned out there was plenty of dead wood in the area; it was just a matter of extending the search far enough to get it. Ashley worked on carving a burning stick by cutting thin layers into a small dry branch and arranging wood chips. She put a match to them, breathed carefully, and watched a small flame try to burn. She protected the tiny flames and carved more chips from the driest limbs in the pile. Before long, the flames consumed the chips and began to flicker away at the larger pieces. She added more chips and continued to add chips until the larger pieces warmed and sizzled the water out. Then they had a fire. A lesson learned: Dry some wood by placing it next to the fire and then keep it in a dry place until you need it to start another fire. The learning curve had edged upward for the group.

Rick had watched and helped Branch set up two previous camps and decided to find the tarp and cover the community area, including the fire. As he worked on it, he realized that he could do it. It was just a matter of getting started. Jerry and Ben helped him. Nylon cords, stretched from boulders to tree limbs, supported the tarp and kept it far enough away from the flames below. Protection from the dampness improved everybody's mood. The wood pile continued to grow under the roof.

Jim had hired Rick as a camp assistant and full-time paddler. Jim didn't need somebody with wilderness survival skills; he had that with Branch. Rick had a pleasant personality and convinced Jim he could learn whatever new tasks Jim presented him. Rick had finished his first year of college at Washington State in June and decided to work in Alaska through the summer and then get a job on a fishing boat. Then he would go back to school in the spring without having to take out student loans. Besides, he liked the outdoors and thought he would return with some new skills and perspectives. Everybody found Rick agreeable—perhaps too agreeable for his long-term good. A malleable personality made him easy to get along with. That was good for Jim because the guests never found anything to dispute. Even when guests asked him about politics, he escaped without being disagreeable. Just what Jim had wanted for this trip.

With the tarp in place, Sandy and Roberta foraged through the trunks and found cooking utensils and the remaining food supply. They decided on coffee and hot oatmeal for breakfast. They put two pots of water on a grill and waited for it to boil. With adequate wood safely under the tarp they awaited breakfast. While waiting, they marched toward the crumpled ice that consumed Jim, Branch, and the canoes. It was hopeless. Tons and tons of ice. Nobody even considered an attempt to dig into the ice mass.

When they finished the oatmeal, they sat around the fire with some bad coffee. An item they thought they could improve. They discussed their predicament. The only two who knew about the wilderness were gone. They also knew that they were the last scheduled trip down the river for the year. Hunting season had closed two days earlier and they couldn't imagine anybody else coming down the river. They hoped somebody would, but they didn't know.

The fact that it was day four of a planned trip expected to last thirty-three days didn't encourage them. They wondered if a bush plane would have any reason to fly over the river before their scheduled haul-out. Jim had arranged this trip as a special arctic adventure. It offered all participants an opportunity to have the wilderness to themselves. The proposition was that they would be the last travelers down the river. Not only would the season change before their eyes, but they might even see ice form in the river. Jim had anticipated the possibilities. If ice prevented navigation, they would set up an ice camp and wait for the bush plane. If the campers weren't at the designated haul-out, the pilot would fly up the river until he found them.

The campers knew what they were getting into. Each for their own reason eagerly looked forward to an original arctic wilderness experience. Pre-trip checklists emphasized quality equipment and clothes. All the campers heeded that advice and came with more-than-adequate clothes, tents, and sleeping bags. Before global warming, the river regularly froze as early as the end of September. Lately, however, freeze-up waited until as late as mid-November.

They cleaned the dishes and repackaged the food. Then more practical concerns set in. This was bear country. They knew there was bear spray packed away somewhere and they decided they better dig around until they found it. That search proved successful and they agreed that no one should leave camp without a cannister in hand. But that was no problem, because no one wanted to leave camp for a walk, or even photography. In this time of despair, they assumed safety in numbers. Even forays for firewood were made in groups of two or more. They made it through the night and started their third day at the glacial site much like the previous day.

By noon, they hadn't made much progress. Decisions seemed to be frozen in time. A discussion centered on arranging stones to spell out SOS and building a signal fire out in the open in case a plane flew over. One question haunted them. How long would it take for someone to come looking for them if they didn't show up on time? They had at least some of the food for each day of the planned trip. Why not stay put, eat well, and wait it out? Again, Roberta stated the obvious. "What if nobody comes?" Ben said he would rather die actively trying to help himself than slowly starve waiting for something to change. Neither position received widespread support. They couldn't bring themselves to seriously consider their obvious options.

"When you want a vacation on the edge, I guess it's all too easy to fall off, one way or the other—we accepted the risk," Roberta said. The campers looked at her, nobody saying anything in response.

"Let's take an inventory. We need to know how bad this is," Ben said.

"How much food do we have?" Sandy asked.

"Let's dig into it," Jerry said. Dry bags, packs, and trunks were opened, and everything laid out on the riverbank. Good news. Most, if not all, essential equipment was safe. They estimated they indeed had about half the food James and Branch had prepared and packed. Perishables that had been packed in trunks with ice could be repacked. The trunks with ice would be impossible to carry down the river, so they would repack the perishables with ice from the glacier and eat that food first. They repacked the remaining food and supplies late in the afternoon, and that gave them a sense of accomplishment. In the evening, their meal consisted of prepared salad and boiled potatoes, then cleanup, and a seat around the fire.

"We can afford to stay here while we eat the perishable food that would be impossible to carry. After that, we better have a plan of some kind," Roberta said.

That night, each tent considered the advantages and disadvantages of staying or starting down the river. Nobody fully dissected the detailed requirements involved in either plan. They slept and rose with the rhythm of the river. The fire blazed to life and with better, though not good, coffee they watched eggs sizzle near toast on the grill. After breakfast, they carried their coffee cups to the riverbank and only hoped they would see somebody floating down the river. The river offered nothing other than debris and chunks of ice broken loose from the river's surging during the earthquake. That didn't work, so they listened for the engine of a plane. Still nothing.

"We better do something for ourselves," Walt said.

"We can stay here another day or two without wasting any food," Sandy said.

"After that we better have made a decision," Paul said.

Either by maintaining congeniality or despite it, no serious decisions were being made.

During the third day of trekking down the river, Tom found the river campers still with tents set up near the crumbled glacier that confined their dead leaders and canoes.

To the campers, Tom looked the part of the wilderness guide. Dressed in leather and sporting a lot of hair around his face, Tom's hat hid any part of his face the hair didn't hide. They looked for his eyes, but if they were open, they couldn't see them.

Tom analyzed the situation, mainly the missing boats. He walked up to the group and asked them about their rafts. He didn't identify a single individual; he recognized a group of people. At that point, the group represented little more than an out-of-place phenomenon. They didn't belong here. His preoccupation negated any sense of empathy.

One of them spoke to him. Jerry told him their canoes and two people, the expedition leaders, were buried under the ice. Tom asked what they planned to do; Jerry said he didn't know. Tom told them they better make some decisions before the weather changed. Then he repositioned his pack and started down the river.

"Can you help us?" Paul shouted out.

"I've got my own problems," Tom said in a voice intended more as a thought than a statement to the strangers. He continued hiking at a steady pace without looking back. Everyone on the gravel riverbank stared silently until he was out of sight.

"He seemed to have a plan. Maybe we better figure something out," Ben said. Ben looked over to Walt, who nodded his head.

"Let's see if we can get agreement on a plan. Arguing here isn't going to get us home," Walt told his partner. "Hey, everybody, let's meet over here to make some decisions." The people gathered around Ben and Walt.

"We need a plan we can all agree on. Before we can decide, we should explore all our options," Roberta said.

"That's right. Option one could be to stay right here," Jerry said.

"Or, we could pack up and follow that guy," Rick said.

"I don't want anything to do with him," Paul said. His wife, Sandy, agreed.

"You don't have to like him. Maybe we should consider his knowledge and abilities," Ashley said.

"Looked to me like he was in survival mode," Walt said.

"He's likely got skills and abilities beyond most of us," Roberta said.

A mostly civilized discussion continued for almost an hour until they narrowed their options to either staying put and starting a fire on the gravel bank or packing up and following the river. Because they had only half their food, they decided to leave. That meant putting things in order. Ben organized a method of assessment. They opened all packs, dry bags, and boxes, then they combined similar items in clusters aligned on the ground. They couldn't afford duplication and excessive weight.

Food and shelter were the essentials. They agreed to select contents of their packs by committee. Sleeping bags and tents were the first items in each camper's keeper pile. A change of clothes plus extra socks added to the mix. Accepted kitchen equipment included two pots, a frying pan, a grill, cups, plates, and flatware. Everyone kept a pocketknife in their pocket or a hunting-style knife on their belt. The medical kit, hatchet, large tarp, ropes, and cords made the important list.

Paul looked at the piles of rejected equipment. He identified some of over ten thousand dollars' worth of cameras and camera equipment. Oh well, he thought; we've got more important things to worry about than to document our trip down the river.

For food, Paul selected all the dried items first. His reasoning looked to reducing the weight, so he also couldn't see a reason to carry any water. Of course, that decision precluded any bottled water. They would capture rainwater or boil river water for drinking. Everyone would carry their own refillable water bottle. Next, they selected fresh food: potatoes and onions would provide critical nutrition, and they accepted some greens, knowing they would have to eat them first. All the matches were collected and packed in waterproof containers, then they distributed the containers to various campers for safety. The campers, soon to be trekkers, slept fitfully. First thing in the morning, with weight distributed according to abilities, they started down the river.

Ben silently and confidently assumed they made the correct decision, Paul and Sandy, less so. But they all moved together. The procession looked like a team effort. Rick carried Jim's .44 Magnum pistol, and everyone had a cannister of bear spray. They paid attention to daylight and made certain to stop and set up camp in time to collect wood and cook before dark. Their first night on the trail affirmed good decisions, at least regarding supplies and equipment. They were being proactive, and everyone worked well together.

CHAPTER 3

September 27, 2:30 PM

*J*ohnson's single-engine bush plane touched down on the rough and rocky landing strip as it had done twenty times in the last several years. The plane bounced once, but before it came down to earth the second time, the shale bedrock heaved, shifted, and contorted the gravel landing area. The shifting bedrock sent a slab of rock three feet out of position and directly in front of the left landing gear. Ted Johnson never saw it, or anything else. The airplane cartwheeled when it hit the impediment, sending it engine-first into the riverbank. The force of the crash sheared the left wing and sent the remnants careening upside down into the river. The airplane sank almost immediately, spinning in an instantaneous whirlpool. Rocks, ice, and debris, their grip on the near-vertical mountainside broken, slid off the mountain and into the river. The earthquake and resulting rockslides made the water movement especially violent. The fuselage disappeared as the whirlpool sucked it down. The remaining wing spun downward until only the tip remained visible. The wide, deep, and placid stretch of river transformed into a vicious roiling mass—ambiguous and uncontrolled, with no respect for its former borders.

"What the hell?" shouted Eric, as he stumbled on the shaking ground.

"Run, get up here. The river's flooding. Help me drag this head to higher ground," Connor shouted. Eric ran to Connor and helped drag the moose head with trophy antlers to higher ground. With the moose head safely away from the water, Eric and Connor looked out over the river. The whirlpool continued to swirl slowly. The river now consumed the airplane. After several minutes, the river rushed away, exposing the wing tip. As the river continued to heave and pulse, Eric noticed that, except for the wing, the entire airplane was buried under rocks and gravel.

"That's a lost cause," Eric whispered.

"I don't know what the water's going to do. Let's go down there. If the water drops a few more feet, we might be able to get to it." They walked to the water's edge. Then they ran back up the bank as more water rushed in, refilling the river.

After fifteen minutes of undulating water levels, the river stabilized somewhat. Three feet of the wing tip remained above the water.

When the heavy shaking subsided, reality set in—at least, their reality. "Jesus Christ, I wonder if the next plane will be able to land here," Eric said. He took a long look at what moments ago had been an acceptable landing strip. Now there were uneven ripples of rocks, potholes, fluctuating water, and a plane's wing crumpled and littering the riverbank.

Ted Johnson had flown Eric and Connor into the wilderness to hunt. He owned the independent outfitting and bush-plane flight company. And he was independent. He studied wildlife conditions here. He knew every tributary, mountain, and swamp area. He knew where his clients would have an opportunity to find trophy game. His reputation was unmatched, especially with hunters. He had no employees; he booked and served his clients by himself. He charged appropriately, and hunters paid it because he got results. When the river swallowed him, any record of Eric and Connor in the wilderness was gone with him. There was no backup. Only family or friends back in the lower forty-eight would miss them when they failed to return. That fact failed to concern Eric and Connor when they booked the trip. They'd had no intention of advertising where they were or what they were doing anyway.

The two brothers lived off a family inheritance. In their early thirties, they accomplished little more than talking to brokers and spending a lot of time in the gym when they weren't sailing or flying. They owned an expensive sailboat they sailed on Lake Michigan. They also owned the twin-engine airplane they flew around the country when they were bored in Chicago. Now the airplane was tied down in Fairbanks.

Two previous hunting trips to Alaska resulted in a brown bear and a caribou. The moose head they had on the beach would fill an empty space on a wall in the family home among deer and elk heads. Seven days in the wilderness had served them well. They had their moose. An insulated tent, blow-up mattresses, expensive camp ware, and plenty of prepared food kept them comfortable. They wore the best leather boots available, not recommended footwear in this hunting environment. The rest of the wardrobe demonstrated the best wilderness-dress money could buy.

"I guess we're going to have to flatten out that runway ourselves," Eric said.

"Who do you think is going to land on it?"

"Somebody in Johnson's office will get a plane out here."

"Not likely. Remember, he told he us he worked alone because he didn't want everybody to learn what he knows."

"Somebody has to know what he's up to."

"I hope you're right. There will probably be another float group coming down the river too. We'll get them to help. We've already seen a couple of rafters come down the river."

"That might be our best chance. We have to make sure we don't miss them."

Eric and Connor reestablished their camp. After rebuilding their tent and stretching a tarp over their kitchen, they positioned their padded chairs, poured expensive scotch whiskey, and readied themselves to hail possible rescuers as they watched the river heave and wither. Nobody showed up. The river in turmoil didn't seem to register with them.

With the last of the natural light, they lit a gas lantern and heated a prepared meal. They ate, had another whiskey, and went to bed.

They spent the next day watching the river. The second day after the earthquake, they worked all day clearing irregular rocks off the potential runway. They thought it would be an acceptable landing site. Eric and Connor worked hard. They didn't like it but didn't want to risk the health of another rescue plane. On the fourth day, they became seriously concerned. They never liked waiting for service, let alone rescue—this was new to them, and they didn't like waiting any more than they liked working.

"I'd like to do something besides sit and wait. Maybe we should climb that mountain behind us. We could get a better look at the river," Eric said.

"I'd like to do something too, but we can't afford to miss any rafters coming down the river."

"You're right. Next time we do this, we'll have to bring some women," Eric said.

"Yeah, and maybe a cook as well. I'm getting tired of cooking and washing."

"If we don't get out of here pretty quick, we're going to miss our wine tasting in France."

"I could miss that, but I don't want to spend that time here either," Connor said.

"I wonder what Mom and Dad would have thought about this."

"Dad would've claimed he tried to toughen us up for this." Eric and Connor idly reminisced about their childhood and the roles their parents played. "Remember the time when Dad was going to toughen us up by making us dig that tree stump out of the backyard?" Eric asked.

Connor laughed. "If it weren't for Jorge, it would still be there. Dad told us we couldn't come in to eat until we dug it out."

"Lot of good that did—Mom brought us sandwiches out the back door. She finally made him let us in when it got dark. They had a big argument about that."

"Mom said if he wanted tough kids, she'd send us to the gym. He was mad as hell. He said she completely missed the point," Connor said.

"I think the gym was better. We're in fairly good shape."

"He always criticized us, saying we never had the guts to make anything out of ourselves."

"We're doing okay," Eric said as he sipped his whiskey. The seriousness of the situation, to them, was that they had to wait. They effectively ignored the fact that they were on their own.

"Do you think we're in as much trouble as when we crashed that car in South Africa?" Connor asked, with an amount of seriousness in his voice. "You know, that could have turned ugly."

"It was ugly, but they came to get us."

"They came to get us because they knew we were out there. I'm really not so sure anybody knows we're here."

Eric and Connor had been on a photo safari to South Africa to photograph cheetahs, lions, and elephants. A high-quality, high-comfort compound catered to most of their needs. Organized daily forays into the bush with a guide resulted in some excellent action shots of wildlife in their natural environment. They had access to a vehicle for independent local travel. The strong advice each time they used the vehicle was, "Be back at the compound before dark." They listened nonchalantly, but everything they experienced emphasized safety. They felt secure.

To complete their expectations for the trip, they needed one more shot: a sunset photo of a cheetah resting in the branches of a leafless tree. They had identified the tree and had seen cheetahs in that area on one of their previous excursions. They decided to go get the shot.

Eric and Connor listened to the usual advice in the midafternoon sun, and they left the compound with two bottles of water and their cameras attached to large lenses. Eric studied the map they had marked while Connor sped across the savanna. After one wrong turn and a detour over a rocky road and through some rough territory, they found their tree. The sun hung in the sky a hand's width from the tree on the horizon. That meant they had about an hour before the sun would be directly behind the tree. They were able to set up the camera tripods behind low-lying bushes to minimize their visibility toward the tree or any cheetahs. They knew they had made all the right decisions when a cheetah arrived at the tree with a fresh kill. The cheetah jumped and scaled the tree to a limb that would be perfect for photography. The prize creature positioned his meal into branches that would hold it in place while he began to eat. Eric and Connor clicked away. After hundreds of spectacular shutter cycles, the photographers rejoiced in knowing they had world-class shots of one of the world's most sought-after scenes.

As total darkness closed in, they stowed the equipment and started back. Eric used his flashlight to review the map and questioned Connor about the detour they had taken. They knew the detour would get them back to the compound. They weren't sure about the other fork in the road. Without serious consideration, they decided to retrace the roads that got them to the tree.

After a half hour of bumps and ruts on a very dark night, their vehicle ran into something, causing a crashing stop in a deep rut at the edge of the road. That got their attention. Eric looked to Connor and asked if he'd seen what they hit. Connor said no. After considerable angst, they thought they'd better get out to examine the damage. They found an odd-shaped steel fabrication with sharp spikes welded onto it. One of the spikes had destroyed the right front tire. The left front wheel pointed in a direction inconsistent with the steering wheel. Without major work in a garage, their vehicle was finished.

Eric said he was sure the contraption was not in the road on the way in. Connor agreed. That fact forced them to consider the warnings they had been given about being back before dark. They had to face the fact that something bad could happen. Somebody might show up and try to steal their cameras. Eric said they should get the memory cards with the photographs out of the cameras, because the photographs were potentially more valuable than the cameras. They removed the memory cards and stuffed them in their pockets, then sat in the front seat with the windows up and the doors locked. They knew that wasn't much security, but it might slow things a little.

Within ten minutes, lights appeared on the road ahead. The vehicle stopped, and a blinding high-powered searchlight shone through the windshield and into their faces. They opened the doors and heard voices as the vehicle advanced slowly. When it stopped within a hundred feet, the spotlight focused on their feet, and Eric and Connor could make out two individuals carrying automatic weapons on foot next to the vehicle. A woman called out and asked who they were. Eric answered. The woman said good and asked if they knew how much trouble they were in. Eric said he knew they were responsible for the car. The woman almost laughed and told them that was the least of the problems they could have had. She continued, "There are people in the bushes next to you, and they will kill you if they get the chance." She told them to get in her vehicle and she would get them back to the compound.

"That woman telling us about the dangers in those bushes was a little scary. I still think about it sometimes."

"Yeah, well there are things in the bushes here too. Look up there a hundred yards," Eric whispered.

Connor turned his head to look up the gravel bank toward the trees. "I see him." A large brown bear ambled along the gravel close to the trees, heading downstream. "Is your gun loaded?"

"Yeah, but it's in the tent. Let's watch him and let him leave if he wants to." The bear turned his head toward Eric and Connor once, then disregarded them to make his way down the river. "We better keep our rifles handy while we're here."

When evening approached, Connor went to the insulated chest with food and fumbled through the contents. "I can't say I'm very hungry, you?"

"Can't say I am. Waiting out here has put me off a bit."

"We've got about four more days of meals and some miscellaneous stuff in here. Maybe we ought to try to stretch it out some."

"I think you're right. I'll have scotch tonight."

CHAPTER 4

The air was clear as Tom started out the next day after he met the river campers. He closed his pack, rolled and tied his oilskin coat to it, and followed the river. Tom thought about the campers at the crumpled glacier. Maybe he shouldn't have left them. Then he questioned what he could do for them. Except wait on the riverbank with them, he couldn't think of much he could have done. He didn't think there was any way they could keep up with him. And even if they could, they weren't ready to leave. He thought the best he could do for them would be to send a search party out for them after he got to Fort Yukon.

He dismissed the thought of going back to them and kept walking until he came upon a bear sniffing about near the shore. Tom's instinct instantly told him the bear wasn't ambivalent about him being in her domain; she was ready for breakfast and waded into the river to fish. The bear lunged into the water but came up empty. She whirled, jumped, and made a mighty splash. Still no breakfast, but sooner or later she would catch her fish. Tom assessed the bear's intentions and concluded she would rather fish than fight. Without a worry, Tom watched the bear in the shallow water surrounded by fish. The scene was familiar to him—a five-hundred-pound bear lunging, splashing, and swatting at fast-moving shadows all around. Persistence would pay off.

He decided to go around the bear by again climbing up the side of the mountain. He surveyed the mountainside, took one more look at the bear, and backed slowly down the trail. Tom assumed the bear knew he was in the area, due to the animal's remarkable olfactory senses. But he also knew that a bear wouldn't give up a plush fishing spot without good reason, especially during this time of the year. Putting on a last layer of fat was too important. When he was out of the bear's vision, he took a running step to climb up the steep incline and get off the trail and up the mountainside. In his natural manner, he picked his way up the rough terrain hand over hand until he achieved some flat surfaces.

What Tom didn't see or consider until it was too late was the mother bear's two young cubs. They growled an alarm, and Tom knew he was in trouble. He never had a chance. Before he could get his pack off and draw his knife, the mother bear caught him with a mighty blow that ripped a huge bloody gash on his arm and knocked him back down the mountainside to the trail. Tom's hat went flying and his pack hung from one shoulder. Tom went down, the bear followed, and picked Tom's foot up in her mouth. Remarkably, she didn't complete the bite. Tom made his second mistake. He tried to kick his foot free. The bear didn't like that, and she tightened her grip on his foot and swung him around in a half circle by his foot.

He had been told that a brown bear will usually leave you alone if you don't fight back. He remained still and trusted what he'd been taught, because he was running out of options. The bear stood over him on her hind legs and growled. Tom didn't move. Then the bear dropped down to all fours and sniffed around Tom's head. Tom thought his tactic would either work, or it wouldn't. His patience remained in full force. The bear opened her mouth and Tom felt her teeth on his skull. It was too late to try anything other than hope. The bear didn't crush Tom's skull, but she ripped a large area of his scalp open. Then the bear reared and landed both front feet on Tom's chest. The sudden weight crushed the air from his lungs. She stepped back and watched Tom. He didn't blink. After what seemed like forever, the bear decided this human was no longer a threat to her cubs and herded them across the river, leaving Tom incapacitated on the trail. Something wasn't right in his chest.

Tom passed out and remained sprawled on the trail until the following morning. In the cool morning air, he stirred and fought to open one eye through blood-encrusted eyelashes. He worked to get both eyes open; they both worked. He thought that was good. Then he tried to use his hand. That hurt. The bloody gash on his arm affected the use of his hand. He leaned on his good arm and tried to sit up. That seemed to work, but he felt the pain in his chest. Then he positioned his foot to put some pressure on it. That didn't work. His foot wasn't operational. That worried him more than all the blood. In the wilderness, life depended on mobility.

Tom knew he had to stop the bleeding, but faintness overtook him, and again he passed out. Tom was in serious trouble alone in the wilderness, with considerable blood loss and blood continuing to flow. That condition alone could kill most people. Head trauma, chest pains, and immobility produced a nearly hopeless situation. He remained motionless, face down on the trail. No family, no friends, and he had already rejected the only people that even knew he existed out here. Life in the wilderness is uncertain and can be cruel. Sometimes death comes instantly and painlessly, sometimes slowly. Tom's heart continued to pump blood out onto the trail. Now the tables were turned. Tom was in more trouble than even the people he had passed on the riverbank. At least they were operational.

The river campers had early coffee, potatoes, and breakfast meat. The morning activities progressed at an efficient pace. They knew they couldn't afford leisure time. They washed and stowed kitchen equipment, loaded their packs, and left the fire burning.

Paul asked Jerry if he thought they had made the correct decision. Jerry said he thought it was good that they had decided, had made any decision. He added that now they would make the best of it. They talked their way along the river. No bears or other distractions interfered with progress; the wildlife avoided the noisy group. Rick led the group along the trail for five hours nonstop before he spotted Tom.

Ashley dropped her pack and went to the sprawled body. She knelt next to him to check for breathing and a heart rate.

"He's still alive."

"Good for him. We've got our own problems," Paul said, repeating Tom's farewell statement from their first meeting. That crisp remark caught Sandy's attention and she stared at Paul. That didn't sound like something he would blurt out. She didn't necessarily disagree, but it just didn't seem like Paul.

Walt joined Ashley to inspect Tom's wounds. "Get the medical kit, a clean towel, and some water," Walt called out.

"We need to start a fire to boil some water," Ashley said.

Roberta had the medical kit in her pack and brought it to Ashley. Ben went to the river for water. Ashley cautiously dabbed water around Tom's head wounds until she could ascertain the extent and severity of the injuries. She washed the blood and dirt from his bearded face, and Tom opened his eyes. Walt asked Tom if he could understand him. Tom answered with a weak, "Uh huh." Ashley continued to work around the wound on his forehead and scalp. It extended from above his left eye for six inches over the top of his head. Obviously, the wound needed sutures. No emergency room with supplies out here. She opened the blade of her pocketknife to cut hair away from the wound but didn't use it. Ashley thought the effective doctoring would require everything available to close the wound.

"How bad is it?" Tom asked, still with a weak voice.

"I can't find any crushed skull bone or puncture wounds. I think I can clean this up. You've lost a lot of blood. Can you sip some water?" Ashley asked.

Tom finally realized that the people helping him were the people he had left on the river. "Why are you trying to help me?" he asked.

"You need it," Ashley answered.

Tom closed his eyes and exhaled. He knew he was in trouble, but he wasn't used to accepting help from anybody.

Ben poured a cup of water for him. Walt helped Ashley apply antiseptic to the head wound. Then Ashley twisted lengths of Tom's hair on each side of the wound and tied knots in the hair to hold the scalp in place and close the wound. The hair acted as a good alternative to emergency room supplies. Then Ashley turned her attention to Tom's bloody arm. Walt cut the tattered leather shirt sleeve away and that revealed a nasty linear gash. Again, this wound had let a lot of blood escape.

"We're not going anywhere for a while. Let's get a camp set up, and we can heat some soup for this man," Ben said. Ashley cleaned the arm wound and applied more antiseptic. Walt helped her wrap and immobilize it.

Tom reluctantly said he thought his ankle was broken. Walt removed the boot with bite marks on it and found a swollen ankle with bruises from the bite. Tom winced when Walt touched it. Walt told him to hang in there because he had to know if it was broken or dislocated. Walt grasped the sole of Tom's foot and moved it around in a circular motion to determine damage. He said he thought it was a bad sprain, not broken or dislocated. In any case he wasn't going to do any walking on it for a while. Walt replaced the boot and laced it to provide some minor support.

Tom regained most of his senses and returned to his practical mode. "If you have a gun, you better be ready to use it when you go down that trail."

"What happened to your gun?" Paul asked.

"I lost mine in the quake, and all the rest of my family's guns were burned up in the fire."

"What fire?" Paul asked.

Tom decided to answer their questions. All he could muster was a weak voice. Maybe somebody would care how he died. "The quake collapsed our cabin, which killed my parents and spread the fireplace flames until they burned everything. Now I've got to get out of here by myself." Tom neglected to tell any of them about the pain in his chest.

"Yeah, we've all got our problems," Paul said and backed away.

Away from the doctoring, Paul and Sandy had a discussion with Rick. They didn't bother to lower the tone or volume. Sandy wanted to know when they could continue down the trail. Rick was worried about more bears or other problems. Paul made it clear that because Tom had left them on the riverbank, they didn't owe Tom anything. Paul and Sandy pressured Rick and tried to get him to consider moving on soon.

Ashley left Walt with Tom and joined the discussion. She didn't like the pressure from Paul and Sandy, but she remained silent. Jerry and Roberta sat on a rock and analyzed the motives and actions of the two camps. Jerry and Roberta knew they weren't going to leave Tom alone in his condition. It wasn't something they could even consider.

Ben and Walt helped Roberta repack the medicine kit and store it in her pack. Ashley asked when Tom would be able to travel. Walt said he wasn't going to be walking for several days. The only way he could leave would be on a stretcher.

Ben sat down next to Tom and tried to talk to him about both his health and the situation in general. Tom was reluctant to share anything. It appeared to Ben that Tom was aware of Paul and Sandy's desire to leave him. Tom's combative demeanor cut Ben's interrogation short.

Ben, Walt, and Ashley joined Jerry and Roberta. Roberta asked about Tom and whether they should stay here with him or take him with them, or whether Tom would even accept the help. Ben told her he didn't think Tom was in a condition to make that decision for himself.

Walt said Tom couldn't travel by himself. Jerry asked Paul, Sandy, and Rick what they thought. Sandy wanted to know when they could get started. Paul said he and Rick had discussed it and wanted to get away from the bear's fishing area.

"If we leave soon, we'll have to put Tom on a stretcher and carry him," Walt said.

"Tom may not accept help," Ben said.

"Then we'll have to leave him," Sandy said.

"That's not going to happen," replied Ashley. Rick listened to Ashley and questioned any of his willingness to side with Paul and Sandy.

They decided to stay in camp, share some food with Tom, and make decisions in the morning.

Paul felt a cold shiver run down his spine. Then nausea set in. He stepped aside and found a rock seat away from the campers. He shook his head and closed his eyes, trying to squeeze out bad thoughts. He hung his head and tried to put everything in perspective. The current predicament perplexed him. He never imagined his life would come to this. He was reacting like a spoiled brat; he had allowed Tom's dismissal of the group the day before to hurt his feelings.

He managed his life, risks, and rewards. The most dangerous risks of the wilderness had never entered his mind. Now he lived it. He knew the way out would test personal stamina and physical strength. He knew his physical fitness gave him an opportunity to survive. He wouldn't lay down and die. But his internal struggles overwhelmed those considerations. He questioned his personal philosophy. He didn't like giving in to the base thoughts he had about leaving Tom. Those thoughts disgusted him, which led him to consider who he was or who he wanted to be. Back in Cleveland, the idea of leaving someone in need would never have entered his mind.

Paul recollected a time when he witnessed a traffic accident on a country road on his way to a men's retreat that he had an investment in. He stopped and provided medical assistance that saved a life. He transported the bloody victim in his new BMW. The doctor at the hospital told him he'd done the right thing. He missed the retreat but felt good about what he'd done.

So why was the traffic accident victim any different than the situation with Tom? After a time, he concluded that the current concern involved his own mortality. He questioned whether he was afraid to die. Apparently, that came into play. Not only that; it precluded every other concern.

Finally, he shook his head at himself. He decided that his mortality didn't trump common decency and concern for fellow travelers. He didn't know how he could ever make it up to Tom, or equally as important, to his fellow campers.

Ashley approached Paul, still in deep thought. "Are you okay?" Ashley asked.

He sat up straight, then stood to face her and looked her in the eyes. "Thank you for caring for Tom. I was wrong. I was wrong, I want you to know that. You showed me who you are and I'm proud to know you. From now on, I'll work with you and do whatever I can for Tom." Paul's words stumbled out of his mouth awkwardly, but he was serious, doing his best to make sure Ashley understood that he meant it.

It seemed to Ashley that Paul had reconciled his recent actions with more humane feelings. "Thank you. We'll get out of this."

They walked back to the group together. Then Paul took Sandy aside and explained his revelations and that they had to work for the good of the entire group. "Surviving by sacrificing morality isn't worth it. If we're going to die, it would be with dignity."

Sandy listened carefully. Once she put Paul's thoughts into perspective, she agreed and hugged him. That was the man she had married.

The group appreciated Ashley speaking to Paul. They were pleased to have Paul, Sandy, and Rick back in the group.

In the morning, Tom was less combative, more lucid, but still not overly friendly. Roberta summarized his situation. "Tom is part of the wilderness. Fiercely independent, and not used to accepting help. And he expects everybody else here to be the same. In the wilderness, that attitude might make sense."

That statement added to everyone's rapidly building sense of insecurity. Jerry addressed their vulnerability in the wilderness. He confided that even if they had to carry Tom, his knowledge would outweigh the inconvenience.

They decided to convince Tom to come with them. He was reluctant. He agreed only after Paul went to him, apologized, and told him they were all better off together. Ben and Walt constructed a stretcher and gingerly loaded Tom onto it. The group started down the river, carrying bear spray at the ready, and a .44 Magnum pistol that none of them knew much about.

They stopped on a wide sandy stretch of riverbank. Walt asked Tom how he was doing. "No complaints," was Tom's reply.

Ashley brought trail mix and water for Tom and told him to eat and drink all he could because he had to rebuild his blood supply. Ben sat next to Tom and asked if there was anything he needed. Tom told him, "Nothing unless you can fix my foot." Paul told him patience was going to be the best medicine for that.

Following that short lunch break, they trekked on down the river without incident until the sun dropped low in the sky. A crude campsite and a quick fire made a home for the night. Paul went to Walt and asked if they should help Tom off the stretcher for some personal attention. Walt was surprised by Paul's concern but agreed. Ashley asked Sandy if she could find a package of soup that would help rebuild Tom's health. Sandy complied, heated up the soup, and brought it to Tom, and he thanked her. Ashley asked Tom whether he would rather sleep in the open, have her build a roof over him with a small tarp, or sleep in her tent. He saw just a few high clouds in the sky, so he chose to sleep outside with his tarp.

The next day opened damp, but when the sun rose, everything would dry. Coffee and oatmeal got everybody's engines running. Tom's appetite was better, and he asked for seconds. Paul recognized the good news and brought it to him.

The campers packed up and started down the river. They proceeded, with Tom on the stretcher, over a narrow strip of gravel close to the river. Steep cliffs and mountainsides thick with brush and tall trees kept them near the river. Late in the morning, the riverbed widened, and they spread out onto a rough wide field of gravel.

CHAPTER 5

The river campers carried Tom toward the bush-plane's partial wing and pieces littering the riverbank. A mere curiosity at first. Then they noticed the pieces weren't weathered, and a wing tip stuck up out of the river. When the campsite and two campers registered, the trekkers pieced together a tragedy.

Assuming they had been rescued, Eric and Connor shouted out to greet the group. That warm goodwill greeting chilled considerably when they recognized their supposed rescuers as a ragtag bunch with an injured man on a stretcher. Rick, Jerry, Ben, and Walt carried the stretcher with Tom up the riverbank to Eric and Connor. Ben's first question was about the bush plane. Connor explained how the riverbank erupted and the river swallowed the plane. Then he described how the river rose and flooded the crash zone for well over a half hour. Eric said they were waiting for another plane to come in to get them.

Tom said there wouldn't be another plane. He recognized the plane from the red color and the numbers he could see on the wing section. He told them Johnson was a solo operator and didn't joint-mission with anybody. He said he expected that nobody knew they were even missing.

Eric and Connor stared at each other and remained tight lipped. That was the confirmation of what they knew but refused to acknowledge. They had no concept of any means of escaping the wilderness without help. After taking visual stock of each of the river campers and long looks up and down the river, Eric got around to asking about Tom. Tom said it was a bear and that he would be just fine. Ben asked how Eric and Connor were going to get back to civilization. Eric and Connor looked at each other and again, remained silent. Their self-confidence slowed, unsure of their next move. A closer inspection of what a bear had done to Tom turned them an even lighter shade of pale.

Tom's condition proved how naively vulnerable Eric and Connor were and how they had failed to appreciate it. With few exceptions, the adventures of their active lives were measured and insured with the best equipment, supplies, and guides. They liked to play the great world explorers, but it was always play. They usually actively avoided putting their lives on the line. But like the one other venture that had landed them in jeopardy, this situation was turning serious.

The intention for this trip to Alaska was to camp out by themselves, kill a scouted moose, and return with a trophy. Until the earthquake, the basic plans were working. They had their trophy, and expensive camp equipment lined the riverbank. Strategically organized meals and good liquor completed their needs. Now, everything changed. Unlike their African problem that they willingly walked into; the current predicament caught them completely off guard.

They walked off a few paces and dug deep to consider their options; what they most needed was a viable rescue. Now they were faced with a group of people that looked as vulnerable as they were. So, they could stay put and let the trekkers pass through. That didn't seem like a good option. These people were their first contact since Johnson, their now-dead guide, had tried to return to bring them back from the river.

But perhaps if they joined the group, they could exert some amount of preferred status. It was worth an attempt. They would still have access to any rafters who came up to them as they made their way down the river. A quick calculation made it obvious that they had little to lose by joining up. Even if another airplane came to their camp, surely, they would still be found even if they were further down the river.

Sandy interrupted the trekker talks and asked if they were going to stop and camp here or try to make a few more miles today. Jerry said it appeared that Eric and Connor were in the same position as they were and suggested they consider a consolidation. When the other trekkers nodded in agreement, Ben stepped forward to ask: did Eric and Connor want to join them on the trek down the river?

Connor said they probably should give that some serious consideration. He said they had some high-quality camp equipment, and that they would want to bring their trophy moose head and hide. If Tom's facial condition would have allowed it, he would have laughed out loud. He managed an "Oh shit."

Walt made it plain and in simple English. If Eric and Connor joined them, the baggage would be necessities only, adding, "We're in trouble here."

Connor explained that they had spent a lot of time, money, and effort to get their moose. Paul sided with Tom and told Connor what he thought Tom would want to say. "Why don't you stay here and die with it, then?"

Connor motioned for Eric to follow him a few steps away. After some whispering, they returned and asked how they would decide on what to bring. Jerry said they could sort through their supplies and select what would supplement the needs of the group. For the rest of the afternoon, negotiations and minor arguments ensued over equipment and supplies.

By daylight, decisions still had not been finalized. Ben went to Tom and said, "Look, I know you are the only one who knows how to get out of this alive. Are you strong enough to help make the life-and-death decisions? I can be your voice and right-hand man until you can take physical control yourself."

Tom said, "I think your idea is the only way Eric and Connor will ever make it out. If you can control the group, I'd be willing to have the new guys join, but I won't put up with any bullshit."

Ben called a meeting. He asked everybody to sit, including Eric and Connor, while he explained survival requirements and Tom's demands. Ben made it clear that Tom was the only one that had the knowledge that would make the difference between life and death. He emphasized that he was talking about life and death. Ben explained that Tom would be the undisputed expedition captain and he would be acting for Tom until Tom was strong enough to take over.

Paul and Sandy seldom surrendered total control, but they quickly agreed. Eric and Connor, however, asked for some special considerations before they would agree.

Ashley told Eric and Connor that they hadn't taken any management actions so far and thought they should learn to follow some effective leadership.

Walt put it more bluntly. "You two need to decide right now—stay put or take orders with the rest of the group. Choose."

Eric and Connor quietly agreed to take orders.

Ben returned to Tom and told him they had agreement. Tom said that was good. He told Ben they would have to assign jobs and responsibilities. He asked if anybody was competent with food—storing, packing, preparation, and cooking. Ben told him Paul and Sandy owned a restaurant and seemed to know their way around food. Tom told Ben to put them in charge of food and that they should immediately select what they would need for the next two weeks.

Tom then asked who could be responsible for health. Ben said that Walt and Ashley seemed like reasonable delegates. Ashley had performed or been a victim needing many of those tasks in her youth on a cattle ranch. Tom told Ben he wanted to talk to them about checking each person for adequate footwear and clothes.

Jerry and Roberta were charged with safety and security. Rick was charged with campsite management and fires. Eric and Connor would be responsible for hunting and emergency use of the rifle. Beyond that, they were assigned to be available for immediate needs when unanticipated tasks cropped up. When anybody required additional help, Eric and Connor carried the responsibility to redirect their efforts in order to help.

Tom and Ben interviewed each of the appointees and explained why and how their responsibilities were critical for survival. Tom secured commitments regarding every assignment. He emphasized to each of them that their assigned responsibilities would all be critical.

"If any of your responsibilities appear to be in jeopardy, I need to know about it immediately. Tell me," Ben said affirmatively.

Tom told Ben that in three or four days they should be out of the canyons. The steep wooded mountains would be behind them and the river would flatten out where they should be able to build a boat and float out of the wilderness. He advised Ben that he should keep that information to himself. Tom wanted Ben to assure that all waterproof materials got packed and protected. He also gave instructions to Ben about the moose.

Ben went to Eric and Connor and instructed them to carefully carve the moose hide into a single strip one-half-inch wide. He emphasized that it could be critical to their survival. Eric and Connor took the directive seriously and began the task without questioning.

The next morning, they loaded the packs. The gravel bar was littered with expensive equipment and a possible top twenty moose trophy that would be left behind. Eric and Connor were silent and aloof. They started down the river. Eric carried his .375 Magnum rifle. Connor's rifle remained with the excess equipment on the riverbank.

The full group's first day down the river was relatively straightforward—no bears, no river crossings, and no extensive brush to cut through. Midafternoon, they approached an open area on the gravel riverbank. Tom asked Walt, who was taking a turn on the stretcher, to have Ben replace him and to get Rick to come to the stretcher. Tom told Ben and Rick to take him to a gravel bank above the river and call a halt. He then directed Ben and Rick to scout the area for signs of bears, firewood, or anything that didn't look safe.

Ben told the campers to take a break while he and Rick scouted the area. They started off toward the trees. Roberta called out to them, "You better take some of this bear spray if you're going up there alone." Tom smiled.

He then asked for Paul and Sandy to come to him. He told them that the only additional food that would come into their possession would likely be a few salmon and that the food they had would have to last up to two weeks. They assured him they would make up appropriate portions.

When Rick returned, Tom told him to take the hatchet and find a tree branch with a crook in it that he could use for a crutch. Rick went into the brush and brought back a likely stout branch. Tom sat up and finished shaping and sizing it with the hatchet. His skill impressed Rick. Tom handed it back to Rick and reminded him that it was important to take good care of it. Rick took it and tied it back into his pack.

Tom tested his crutch and hobbled down to the fire. He moved slowly and he felt the pain, but he was ambulatory. Walt, naturally concerned about his patient, asked Tom if all the moving parts were working. He also reminded Tom that he shouldn't try to test the ankle yet. Walt thought quickly and told Tom if he wasn't going to accept the stretcher, he had to wrap his ankle. Tom accepted that.

Connor wanted to know why there wasn't more food. Sandy told him they were on a budget. Connor mumbled something about starving. Tom told him to shut up. He wouldn't get any more food than anybody else. Tom told the group they could all help the cooks clean up and prepare for breakfast. He also reminded them to clean everything well. They couldn't afford for anybody to get sick. That concern was important to Tom but unnecessary; Paul and Sandy practiced nutrition management as automatically as they took each breath. Tom scanned the campsite. It looked secure, and plenty of wood occupied a dry spot under the tarp. No serious conversations or even questions broke out around the fire. Everybody sat around the fire and contemplated the situation autonomously.

The enormity of the situation forced Ben to consider other adversities he'd faced. Most of his active childhood memories centered on doting parents, fun-loving siblings, good humor, and honor. Something he rarely allowed himself to delve into came front and center. Hard times, oppression, hunger, and like it was for any poor Black family in Alabama, racism. There was no active racist in this group, though Ben was the only person of color. Perhaps some white privilege would emerge, but he wasn't concerned about it. He was concerned about oppression via natural events, hard times, and hunger.

Ben reflected on hard times during his youth. He passed over physical threats, racist remarks, and denial of service in public places. Problems in Ben's youth were injustices nobody should suffer. But his family couldn't escape those injustices any more than he could simply walk to the door and leave the threat of death in the wilderness. He had learned to live with those injustices.

Ben believed that patience, honor, and education would help relieve those injustices. But that idea was at odds with some of Walt's calls for immediate action. Walt hadn't lived through the death threats that existed in the South, and Ben forgave Walt when he wanted to fight. Ben wasn't passive about racism, but he didn't want to risk the gains he'd made in his own life. On the other hand, if he had to decide between joining an active fight for equality and playing it safe, he knew he would give up his safe life.

Now, here in a life-and-death proposition, there was no time to work it out. Nature provided the challenge. You either solved the problem and responded or you died. This was living in real time. Tom was the ticket out of the wilderness as the supreme commander, and Ben would see that Tom's directives were carried out. Ben hadn't noticed any objections, but he prepared to deal with any problems.

Connor's only thought evolved from his share of the food. He worried whether his share increased or decreased after the consolidation with the larger group. Being a team player collided with his way of life. He went to his tent with that thought.

Tom appeared to be somewhat ambulatory. The food budget policy had been enforced. That act alone, gave the campers confidence that anarchy could be avoided with strong leadership. Again, the campers' day ended on a positive note.

A heavy frost covered everything in the morning. Rick took his responsibilities seriously. He was the first one up, and he stirred the coals in the fire pit and added fresh wood that had been covered. Tom quickly crawled out of his tarp and motioned for Ben to follow him away from the campers.

"There's no emergency," Tom said, "but let's not start a vacation mood. Let's move as soon as we can get organized."

Ben got everybody on task. Ashley queried each of them about the condition of their feet and footwear because Tom made that a top priority for her.

Before the frost cleared, Tom, on his crutch, led the way down the riverbank. Two hours later, they rounded a bend in the river and faced trees and a thick undergrowth that ran from the water's edge all the way up a steep mountainside. Tom told Rick to lead the way into the brush and clear a path. Then he asked Rick if he knew what devil's club was. Rick said he didn't. Tom led everybody toward the brush and pointed out a bush with nasty stinging thorns. "Don't touch it. If we make it through this, you can thank Rick." Tom told Rick to cut a stick to beat the bushes back and down. He also told everybody to carry a stick to help avoid touching the bushes. Tom also assigned the bear spray to Rick. Ben would bring up the rear with more bear spray and a whistle.

The going was slow and tortuous. Despite best efforts, the spiky stinging devil's club got to them. It was early afternoon before they emerged from the undergrowth. Tom told everybody to take a break. They would be uncomfortable for a while, but it wasn't fatal. Connor and Eric complained about the route. Tom sent them out to the perimeter with bear spray to assure they were safe. Tom wanted to talk to Walt and Ashley. He told them to report back to him after they talked to each camper individually to get a reading on their attitudes and stability after their tough morning.

Ashley and Walt went about casually interrogating everyone. Thirty minutes later, they reported back to Tom. First, they shared their general impression of the group—they were tired and uncomfortable. Tom expected that. What he didn't expect was that most of them expressly appreciated knowing that there was a plan and it seemed like they were making progress.

Some individual concerns came to light: Jerry and Roberta were visibly shaken and scared. Paul and Sandy didn't want to talk about anything other than what they had to do. Sandy seemed okay physically, but she was also unnerved, and her voice cracked. Eric and Connor didn't like taking orders, but they didn't want to confront Tom. Walt thought Eric and Connor were intimidated by Tom.

After a few questions, Tom thanked Ashley and Walt, and he hobbled over to Jerry and Roberta. "Get over those nettles yet?"

"Mostly, I think we survived them. How much more like that do we have?"

"There's a small patch just ahead. I'd like to get through it today if we can. Do you think you can make it? I've got a plan. It would be best if we can do it."

Without waiting for an answer, Tom went on to visit with Paul and Sandy. "After tomorrow, I'm hoping to catch some fish. Then we can eat a full meal, wash, clean up, and rest. Are you with me?"

"We're going to do whatever we have to do," Sandy said, almost under her breath. Tom recognized how accurately Ashley and Walt had described Sandy's condition. He was concerned for her and how it could affect the group.

"Everybody appreciates that. Let's get going." Tom left the conversation worrying about how he could help her regain some confidence. He knew she was scared. Few but the strong survived the wilderness. Outstanding physical strength counted toward that, but attitude and mental fortitude often made the difference. He made a mental note to talk to her privately.

Tom had given everybody a chance to catch their breath, but he didn't want to give them enough time to dwell on how they dreaded the devil's club. He told Ben to get everybody ready to move on.

A half hour later, they approached another area of thick brush. Tom told Eric to find a long stick he could use to break the next path through the understory. Tom told Paul to keep the bear spray and take up the rearguard. Connor carried the rifle and followed Eric into the brush. Within an hour they walked out of the understory onto the clear gravel riverbank. Tom told Ben they'd had enough for the day.

Ashley and Walt checked for any health problems, then went to Tom. "Let's have a look at your wounds."

"Do we have enough supplies?" Tom asked.

"We've got what we need for now," Ashley answered. Then she inspected Tom's head. The scalp was still ugly, but medically acceptable. The good news was that the antiseptic was working. "This is looking rather good. I want to keep it wrapped to keep it clean. How's the arm feel?"

"I can feel it when I try to make a fist."

"Let's see it." Ashley removed the bandaging and poked around the open wound. "No infection. I don't know what to do with this. What do you think, Walt?"

"There's going to be a scar."

"I can live with a scar."

"I would like to put it in a sling to immobilize it, but it would make walking through rough territory more difficult."

"I don't want a sling."

"I don't want you to be able to rotate your wrist. What if I wrapped a stick with your arm down to your fingers? You'd be able to use your fingers and your arm and hand would be stable."

"You've got me put back together so far."

"I don't know how bad it is, but whenever you move your hand, you're destroying any healing. I think we should immobilize it." They did it.

Rick went to work preparing the campsite and starting a fire. Paul and Sandy worked on dinner. All available hands collected firewood.

Tom went to Paul and Sandy's kitchen with instructions for breakfast. He told them he wanted them all to have a quick breakfast in the morning. Then he told them to pack easy-to-eat lunch food near the top of the pack. They wouldn't want to spend too much time preparing or eating it.

Just after sunset, a low mist engulfed the camp. In the morning, everything was wet. Tom got everybody moving at daylight. He knew it would be a long, miserable day, and he thought it would be best if he kept everybody too busy to dwell on it. Sharing his plan with Ben, Tom asked him to prepare to offer encouragement whenever it was needed.

They started down the rough riverbank. The ground was uneven, but clear of brush. The mist turned to rain. Tom kept them focused.

After an hour in the rain, they approached another major test. A thick understory grew into tall trees and continued straight up tall steep bluffs. Again, there was no way around it. Tom told them the next hour was going to be tough. He also told them that on the other side they would face the possibility of bears fishing in a tributary. He told Rick he wanted him to take the lead and that Ben would be with him, carrying the bear spray. Eric and Connor would walk at the end of the line, watching for any activity behind them. Nobody complained, but they weren't smiling, either.

As promised, the trek through the understory was miserable. The trail followed a course of boulders that were mostly hidden by low-lying brush. Devil's club crowded the pathway and overhung it in many places. The slippery boulders often caused the trekkers to find themselves off the trail and either into the water or into a clump of stinging nettles. Between the nettles and the slippery trail, more than a few descriptive phrases were issued. When they emerged onto the gravel riverbank, everyone was exhausted and miserable. Tom told them they did a good job. He also told them to keep their voices down until they surveyed the area for bears. Then he told them to take a well-deserved break. He ordered up an early lunch and they dispersed to eat.

CHAPTER 6

Tom hobbled across the gravel to Paul and Sandy. "Sandy, let's take a little walk."

Sandy looked up from her slumped seat on the gravel bank. She frowned as she looked up to Tom. Tom extended his hand to help her up. She looked to Paul, who nodded. She took Tom's hand and he leaned back on his good foot, gingerly pulled her upright, and guided her toward the river. They walked slowly to the water's edge where they could have a private conversation. The river provided a quiet, peaceful setting. Although the stinging devil's club clung to the mountainside in proximity, it also provided an interesting color contrast to the rest of the varied green shades all the way up the mountain. Tom nodded at the devil's club. "That last stretch was tough, and I don't blame you for hating it. Nobody liked it. But I've accepted a responsibility to get everybody out of here. And that's a job I've never had before. I'm used to being responsible for myself. This is new to me. So, I suppose we're both in somewhat uncharted territory." Tom thought that if he displayed some vulnerability, it would be easier for Sandy to hear him.

Sandy hesitated and finally spoke in a soft, uncertain voice. "Yeah, this is a little different than what I thought I signed up for. I'm used to having a support system back home."

"I understand that. My parents were my support group. But part of that support was preparing me to take care of myself. They never trained me to be a group leader or wilderness guide."

"You seem to know what you're doing."

"I know how to survive. I'm trying to figure out how to make everybody survive. I don't know if you can see it, but that adds a lot of pressure. I don't want to put any pressure on you either, but I need you to be strong. I need you and Paul to manage our food. I can't manage everything. I need you to do it."

It worked. Tom's openness allowed Sandy to speak freely in full voice. "That makes sense. I know food."

"I understand you have a big restaurant back home. Tell me about it." Tom wanted to help Sandy help herself by talking about something she knew.

Sandy began by telling Tom about how they started. "Paul and I wanted to get married and run our own business. We considered everything from building canoes to wholesaling musical equipment. We came here to try our hand at paddling a canoe. Anyway, we settled on food because it was something everybody had to have. We figured if we did a better job of providing it, we would do okay. We did well from the start. We had saved enough money and studied enough to avoid problems a lot of small businesses fail from. There's a lot more to it than shouting short orders through a hole in the wall. We hired good people. In the beginning we also did a lot of the setup and cleanup and everything in between. We didn't have any other responsibilities, so sixteen-hour days didn't bother us. We could see things growing and our debt decreasing. It was during that time that I also partially forgave my alcoholic parents."

Sandy noted Tom's attention, so she continued. "I never asked any of our employees to do anything I haven't done myself. Everything from buying fresh vegetables to cleaning the toilets. When I assign responsibilities, I know what I'm talking about." Then Sandy halted abruptly and stared into Tom's eyes. After several seconds, and still with intent eye contact, she continued, "I see now why everybody is beginning to trust and follow you. You never ask any of us to do something you haven't done yourself. And you'd probably do it all yourself if you had the time and didn't have the injuries."

"That's kinda my point. I've never had to worry about food for more than me and my parents. There's more to this situation than I've ever dealt with on my own. I hope I can depend on you. I hope I'm not adding too much pressure on you and Paul. Have you two always worked together?"

"Yes. Paul's a great partner and still my best friend. I hope you can forgive us for our comments back there. That's not who we are."

"I know that. None of us were in our right minds back there, at least not most of us. Now our job is to get us back on track. I think we can do it. You and Paul must have suffered some hard times at the restaurant."

Sandy agreed and told Tom about losing some good employees. "I had to go back to waiting tables and Paul doubled as a busboy. Both of us did janitorial services. That was tough. We laughed about it later."

"You'll laugh about this later, too."

"I hope so."

"I want you to think about your support group back home. I know that out here you don't get to pick and choose that support but look to your fellow campers and try to let them help you fulfill your psychological needs. I think as a group, we have most of what we need."

"Like any business venture, make the most of what you have."

"That's a good thought."

"I'll try to be strong next time we come to those sticker bushes."

"I think we're through with them."

"Good."

"Tell me what you expected on this trip."

Sandy started with a chance to learn to paddle a canoe. "Paul and I wanted to see what we missed out on when we selected a restaurant over building canoes. Jim advertised the trip as an extended wilderness photo safari. The plan was to live in the wilderness for thirty-some days, watch the weather change, and experience what early gold seekers found. That all changed with the earthquake. Jim and Branch are dead, and we lost the canoes."

"Your expedition was well prepared. You've got good equipment, good clothes, and supplies. That means a lot out here. So, other than the initial trauma, where does that leave us?"

"Right here on the river with no canoes."

"If we could ride down the river, would you feel better about getting out?"

"Of course I would."

"I'm sure Jim and Branch set up campsites, cooked, and cleaned up for the group. If we share those responsibilities, I think we can solve that problem. That's part of what I wanted to talk to you about. I need everybody to share and work on distributed tasks, and in the end, work together. If we can discard the trauma, and if we had the canoes back, would you say we would be close to where you were before the earthquake?"

Sandy looked Tom in the eyes. When she looked away, she thought about being in the wilderness—tents, sleeping bags, fires, cooking, and clothes.

"I think we've got most of what we started with. You're the only one with injuries."

"I think I'm going to be okay. Do you think you can help replace what you lost in Jim and Branch?"

"I'll do what I can."

"That's all anybody can ask." Tom turned and faced the river. "I'm not ready to share this with the group because I don't want to disappoint everyone if I'm wrong, but I think we're going to get some fresh fish, and as importantly, I think we can build a boat to float us out of here. We'll know just a little further down the river."

"We're going to build a boat?"

"Unless a lot of things have changed, that's my plan."

"Well, let's go!"

"Let's go slow and see what happens."

Sandy smiled. It felt good.

CHAPTER 7

Tom led the group down the river for another fifteen minutes until the trees and nonthreatening brush gave way to light, open terrain where they could see a tributary entering the river. And, as Tom expected, a bear was busy wading around, chasing dark darting shadows. The stream entered the river in a wide delta type of area with no cover. The bear fished by himself out in the open, lunging and splashing. Tom suspected the bear wasn't comfortable being exposed like that, even if he was catching salmon.

Tom had a plan. They would chop some pitchfork-like limbs from trees in the thicket, scare the bear away, pitch a dozen salmon onto the bank, string the fish on a pole, and carry them two miles down the river away from the bear's fishing hole. Tom showed Ben and Rick the type of limbs he wanted and sent them off to craft four pitchforks. They returned with adequate weapons to do their fishing. Tom then explained how they would circle around to the other side, downstream from the bear, and chase him up the tributary, away from where the campers wanted to go. Eric loaded his rifle and Tom took the pistol. Ben, Rick, and Walt carried the bear spray. If the bear didn't move away from them, Eric had instructions to fire a warning shot. If that happened, they would know more about the bear's intentions.

Everybody stayed close together and waded into the small stream where it emptied into the river. The bear was less than a hundred yards away. He caught a salmon and held it in his teeth. When the bear noticed the people in the stream, he stood on his hind legs and continued to hold the fish in his mouth. Tom shouted, "Hey, bear." The bear dropped down onto all four feet and ran away, just like Tom had planned.

Without the bear occupying their full attention, they noticed the ingredients for part two of the plan. Things were working. The rain continued and everybody was tired, but they were delighted to complete Tom's plan. Rick, Ben, Connor, and Walt took their makeshift pitchforks into the stream, and within fifteen minutes they had twelve fat salmon on the bank. Ben helped Rick run a long stout limb through the gill and out the mouth of each fish. With the fish mounted, Ben and Rick put the ends of the limb on their shoulders and continued the trek down the river with the group.

The fishing success gave Tom confidence that he could succeed in getting the group to safety. He had caught fish like that before. He had assumed they would catch the fish. He also knew things changed year to year. He was thankful his plan succeeded.

Two miles down the river, Tom pointed out a campsite and told the group they would camp there for three or four days. While Rick organized requirements for the campsite, Tom took Ben for a short walk along a seepage in the sandy fine gravel, not quite enough water to flow freely. After a hundred-yard trek onto higher ground, Tom smiled. They gazed upon the source of the seepage, a large pool with mist rising from the water. Tom walked to the edge and dipped his hand. "Try it."

Ben dipped his hand in the warm water and smiled. Then he asked, "Is this safe for a hot bath?"

"I use it every time I come by here. And I've never seen a bear here. We'll keep a watch anyway. Let's just take a walk around here, to make sure there are no bears." There were few places near the campsite and the pond where a bear could want to be, but they took the time to walk the area. On the way back to the campsite, Ben picked up an armload of firewood.

Standing on the gravel bar, Ashley surveyed the campsite and surrounding area. On the opposite side of the river, a grand rock face rose over two-hundred feet, separated from the river by a small gravel spit. The rock face's peak gave way to a gentle rise with a lightly wooded area leading back and away to much larger mountains. The rock face intrigued her, almost invited her. Any other time, she would have found a way to climb it.

Tom told his charges about the hot pond, and that after they had finished all the setup tasks, including building and starting up a smoker, they could take a dip. First, he wanted a lot of firewood and a big fire. Then he explained the plan to build a rock smokehouse to cure the fish. He designated Ben, Walt, Eric, and Connor to build it. Paul, Sandy, Jerry, and Roberta would clean the fish and save all the salmon eggs. Tom showed them how to slice the fish and coat the pieces with sugar. The fish would start to cure overnight. They set up their tents and stretched a tarp over a common area.

Eric and Connor contributed to the effort with energy and efficiency. They worked in concert with each other and interacted with Ben and Walt as little as possible. Eric and Connor understood the essential nature of the project but didn't like forced labor. Their reticence told everybody they expected deliverance. They didn't like the thought that their money wasn't going to buy them out of this situation.

Light began to disappear when Jerry recognized a boat coming up the river. He quickly called to the group and walked to Tom. Everyone gathered on the riverbank to greet their rescuers. They waved and called out as the boat approached. Three young rough-looking men guided their jet boat close to the shore and idled the engine.

One of the men said, "I'll take the blonde."

Tom whispered to Eric and told Rick to bring the pistol. Eric started toward his tent to retrieve the rifle. Tom stepped forward, ready to confront the men.

"How long you going to be here?" another young man shouted, then tilted a beer can to his mouth. Rescue was not at hand.

Tom decided to stall until the guns arrived. "We'll probably be here a few days. Why?"

"We want the squaw bath."

"You can have it when we leave."

"We want it now."

Given the introductions, sharing the pond would never be a possibility. Tom knew he couldn't allow them to set foot on the bank. Strength would prevail. "Can't have it now."

"It better be first thing in the morning or we'll help ourselves."

Roberta took that as a threat directed at more than just leaving. Rick ran to Tom and handed him the pistol. Eric was close behind. Tom held the pistol pointed toward the ground, but in plain sight.

"I think you should leave," Tom said in his calm, clear voice.

"I'll tell you what we'll do. We'll camp over there tonight. If you're not moving out first thing in the morning, we'll be back to help ourselves," the largest and overweight young man shouted. He lifted a large rifle from the boat. "We've got some of those too." That ended the discussion. The young man at the controls revved the engine unnecessarily and shifted into forward, and the boat jumped and sped to the opposite shore. The young men carelessly ran the boat up onto the gravel spit and unloaded a few cases and their guns. They were undeniably preparing to spend the night.

"What are we going to do?" Jerry asked.

"We're staying. We don't have any other option. This is where I planned to build a boat. We need to smoke the fish and we need to rest. No. We're staying," Tom answered.

"I think you're right. How do we protect ourselves?"

"The worst case will be a shootout. We'll prepare for that; we'll build ourselves some fighting advantages."

"I suppose we can build some bunkers on high ground and make it difficult for them to land," Ben said.

"Just when we start to believe we can survive the wilderness, we run into another fight for our lives," Sandy said.

"When the alcohol wears off, we may not have to do anything, but let's prepare for it," Roberta said.

Tom led the suppressed troupe back up the gravel bank to the camp. Tom paid attention to Sandy's and Roberta's composure. He recognized a lack of unresolved fear; rather, they were angry. He was pleased that Sandy would fight. Ashley watched the landing on the opposite shore and saw undisciplined and uninhibited young men. If it came to a fight, she felt confident. Paul and Jerry remained close to Tom, ready to carry out his directives. Ben and Walt surveyed the area to prepare a battle plan.

"We could shoot them and take the boat," Connor said.

"That's one good plan, but I think we better have substantial provocation. Murder one could land us in a position worse than hunger," Paul said.

"If they try to land on this side of the river it would be enough for me," Eric said with bravado.

"Have you ever killed anybody?" Ben asked. There was no answer.

"Okay. If they try to land right here in front of us, we'll try to talk first. If that doesn't work, it might get drastic." Tom stood directly in front of Eric and in a strong voice, demanded an answer. "Eric, are you sure you can shoot them if it comes to that?"

Eric was taken aback and forced to think out his answer. "I . . . I . . . yes, to protect us, yes I can do that."

"Sleep on it. You may not get much time to think about it tomorrow. Before we go to bed tonight, we'll dig out bunkers so they can't see us from the river. We'll be able to see them, but we'll be invisible. If they take the boat up the river, we'll go up to meet them. If they go down the river, we'll have a harder time defending our positions. Let's get something to eat and share some more strategies. It looks like a clear night and we should be able to monitor them from here. We'll take turns standing watch."

Paul and Sandy configured a quick meal, and the group, minus Rick who was assigned the first guard duty, sat around the fire, sharing ideas.

"I've never fired a gun at anybody, but I suppose I can, if it comes to that. Unless somebody has some military combat training, I'll use the pistol and Eric will use the rifle. The rest of you will arm yourselves with bear spray, sharp sticks, and rocks," Tom said.

"Do you really think they're serious?" Sandy asked.

"We can't take any chances," Walt said.

"When alcohol and testosterone get involved, anything can happen," Roberta said.

"I've seen the results of some bad bar scenes in Nevada. I never thought I'd see it out here. I guess there are young crazies everywhere," Ashley said. "Some of the results can be pretty not nice. I had to fight my way out of a bar once."

"With a gun?" Roberta asked.

"No, but a broken beer bottle got me safely out of a tense situation."

"After they get good and drunk, what if we went over there and tied them up?" Connor asked.

"Yeah, and then what do we do with them?" Ben answered.

"We take their boat," Sandy answered.

"We won't all fit in the boat," Ben said.

"We could do a shuttle," Sandy said.

"That's grand theft," Paul said.

"You know, they're cowards. How can we scare them out?" Roberta asked.

"What we need is another little earthquake to shake some of that rock face onto them," Walt said.

"Too bad we can't just explain our situation to them and ask for help," Roberta said.

"Not going to happen while they're drinking," Ashley said.

Everyone went silent. They had a plan and it didn't seem like there was anything else they could do, other than wait it out. Ashley stared up into the stars. The rest followed her gaze up into the bright sky for close to a minute.

"What do you think they would do if some of that rock face slid off into their camp, Tom?" Ashley asked.

"I don't know. They're not attuned to the wilderness; they're just up here to do some serious drinking. They might leave for some less-troublesome terrain, although they obviously want the hot pond. Not likely to get an appropriate quake, though."

"I'd like to be more proactive than just waiting for them to come calling for rape, pillage, and plunder," Ashley said.

"Me too," Sandy said quietly but determinedly.

"How about if I put my clothes in a dry bag, swim across the river, climb that mountain, and shower them with a few rocks?" Ashley said.

"My kinda girl," Roberta answered, not actually taking her seriously.

"Might work, but I'm in no condition to help you," Tom said.

"No, in the dark? That would be a rough climb. And, there could be devil's club over there," Jerry said.

"I think it's worth a try. If we can't get up the mountain, all we get is wet and cold," Ben said.

"I wouldn't want anybody over there alone, maybe even without a gun," Tom said.

"I'll go with her," Ben said.

"You're serious," Jerry said.

"I don't know about the gun, but I think it could work. We would have to be light and fast," Ben said.

"Is it okay if we try it, Tom?" Ashley asked.

"It'll be a long night. If they come across the river, we'll have the guns ready. Are you sure you want to do it?"

"I wouldn't have said it if I didn't mean it."

Without another word Ashley went to her tent and found a dry bag large enough to hold jeans, shoes, and sweatshirts for her and Ben. Everyone wished them well. Ashley and Ben walked down the river-bank away from the camp, stripped down, filled the dry bag, and waded into the cold water. When the water depth demanded it, they used the dry bag as a float and quietly paddled across the river. On the far bank, they shivered while they quickly brushed the water off and dressed. They could see the dim light of their friends' fire on the opposite side. More closely, they could see the three young men's fire. More disturb-ing, they could easily make out the loud rough language.

The bright sky enabled them to negotiate silently up the gravel to the side of the mountain. At the mountainside, they found the trees and understory blocking the light, so they had to test every step and handhold as they moved up the mountain. The devil's club didn't grow on this mountainside, but other low-growing brush created some sub-stantial obstacles. After an hour of climbing, they came upon a clearing and leaned back for a rest. A few bruises and scratches, that at other times would have irritated them, were minor concerns. So far, every-thing continued as planned.

"For no reason, when we got to our camp today, I studied this rock face. It appeared to be relatively level at the top of the rock, then it sloped back up to meet the rest of the mountain. I'm hoping my obser-vations were right."

"We'll get there and make something work," Ben said.

After another half hour of careful climbing, they looked across a modest incline that almost certainly led to the top of the rock face. They quietly moved to the rock apex. Ashley had calculated the terrain per-fectly. From their vantage, they observed their modest campfire across the river. They allowed themselves time to watch the firelight reflect off their friends' faces. The plan had to succeed for them. Ben and Ashley considered it their best hope for a peaceful resolution. Almost straight below them, the young men's fire blazed; Ben and Ashley watched them sitting and drinking around it, their voices loud and obnoxious, their language atrocious, vulgar, and threatening.

"Okay, what's the plan? Do we just start pelting them with rocks and branches?" Ben asked.

"Basically, but let's give them some psychology to play with first. Let's gather up all the ammunition we'll need. Then, we'll start with a few small stones. See who can hit the fire first. After that fun, we'll send over a small pile of rubble, and more if needed. Alas, we'll bury them if we have to."

The two warriors gathered pebbles and stones to the size of their fists into segregated piles at the edge of the precipice. In another sorted pile, they stacked larger rocks that would be capable of doing substantial damage. At last they were ready.

"Watch and listen. Try to hit the fire, then listen to them. Let's see how long it takes them to realize the sky is falling," Ashley said.

They knelt at the top of the rock face and Ashley let fly with the first stone. Nothing, no reaction. Ben tried. They heard the stone bounce off something other than another rock. Still no response from the young men. Ashley tried again. Ben tried another stone.

"They're either too drunk to recognize a disaster or we're missing everything. Let's try a handful of rocks over the edge." Ben gathered a handful of pea-sized gravel and let it go down the rock face. That got a reaction.

"What's going on?"

"It's nothin'; don't get nervous."

"Hmmm, they've got nerves. Let's make them get nervous now," Ashley said. She went to a preplanned pile of larger stones and pushed them over and listened for a response.

"Ow. Son-of-a-bitch. That wasn't nothin'." Two of the men stood and moved away from the fire toward the river. They didn't speak as they stared up toward the top of the rock. Ben and Ashley remained unseen as they watched.

"Okay, now let's convince them," Ashley said. Ben pushed a larger pile of the same-sized stones over the edge.

"Ah shit, my leg, I can't move it!"

"That one hit me in the shoulder. We've got to get out of here."

Above, Ashely said, "Now Ben, take a handful of stones and see if you can hit their boat."

Ben heaved a handful of stones toward the river.

"Shit, now they're hitting the boat."

"If that ruins my dad's boat, you're in big trouble."

"Quit crying. Who's going to put me in big trouble?"

"That was what I wanted to hear—insecurity, blame, and divisive comments. Here goes another pile of big ones," Ben said.

The flames in the fire sputtered and embers scattered. An obvious direct hit.

"I took another one on my arm. I'm taking the boat home before we're stranded up here."

"Okay shithead, let's go."

"Help me! I can't walk!"

"Get Tony. I'll start the engine."

The engine roared. Ben and Ashley laughed almost as loud as the noise the engine made. After Tony had been pushed into the boat and his helper shoved the boat into the channel, Ben and Ashley pushed the rest of the rocks over the edge.

The young men in the boat watched the fire disintegrate with embers flying in all directions; one of them landed in the boat. The bright sky enabled the three young men to maneuver the boat downstream at full throttle. Ben and Ashley watched them disappear before they started down the mountain.

"Wow, it worked," Walt said, from across the river.

"That was impressive! Those two are amazing. We'll station guards tonight, just in case. Let's take some fire down to the river to help them get back. Get this fire built up. They're going to be cold," Tom said.

There wasn't anything else to say, so they built up the fire and carried burning sticks to the riverbank. With both fires burning strongly, they waited on the riverbank to greet their heroes.

An hour later—"Ahoy, are our friends long gone?" Ben called from the edge of the water.

"They left at full speed. You were amazing. What can we do to help you cross?" Jerry answered.

"Nothing. We'll do it like we got here," Ashley called back.

"Rick has been watching down the river. I don't think they're coming back," Tom said for reassurance.

Ben and Ashley waded out of the river and stood briefly by the fire, shivering.

"I think we should get in our hot tub," Ashley said.

"Of course, that's what you deserve to get warmed up," Roberta said. Walt took the dry bag from Ben and led the naked saviors to the pond. Ben and Ashley sat in the warm water while everybody else sat near the edge and shared the experience. After some hearty laughter deep into the night, Tom relieved Rick on guard and everybody crawled into sleeping bags, greatly relieved. Walt replaced Tom on guard duty two hours later.

CHAPTER 8

Tom allowed everybody to sleep in. They deserved it. Midmorning, Paul and Sandy sheepishly left their tent and apologized to Tom for not having breakfast ready. Tom told them to forget it—everybody deserved the day off. Late in the morning and after a hot breakfast, Tom told the women they could use the pool first. Roberta said that after all they'd been through, modesty was the least of her concerns. That statement slightly surprised Tom. That would be more practical. He scanned expressions, shrugged his shoulders, and said, okay. Everybody went to the pond together. Ashley told Tom to keep his wounds out of the water. She also said the hot water would be good for his foot.

A leisurely and jubilant time in the hot pond consolidated a can-do attitude.

"If we're going to call this home for a while, we've got a lot of work to do," Jerry said.

"Where do we start, Tom?" Roberta asked.

Tom laid out plans and tasks for the rest of the day. His primary concern for the group was to finish building the double-walled smokehouse they had started the day before. He knew that well-cured fish were critical for the rest of the trip. When they left the hot water, tasks occupied them for the remaining daylight hours.

Salmon caviar for hors d'oeuvres and fresh salmon for dinner were followed by cleanup and a nice fire. The campers were exhausted, relieved, and alert as they sat in a circle around the fire and took stock of each other. The three divergent sources to the group intermingled in the circle. The flames cast flickering shadows on the campers in a way that begged most of them to seek more personal information.

Eric and Connor separated themselves, with Paul and Sandy between them. Eric and Connor were the most homogenous pair in the group. Their only interest in the other group members stemmed from what anyone could do to get them home. Eric stared at Tom and hoped he wouldn't have to take orders from this backwoods hick much longer. Other than Ashley's figure and overall appearance, he didn't bother to consider rational characteristics or personalities of any camper. Connor recognized Tom as their exit ticket and knew he had to cooperate. He understood a connection between Ben and Walt and wondered what brought them here together, but it wasn't really important to him. He noticed Ashley and thought he might try to talk to her, but it was not an intellectual intention.

Sandy's eyes darted from face to face as she tried to determine which one belonged to a capable personality, and how that face would fit into an effective effort to get home. Rick's quiet stare into the fire, interrupted only by quick glances around the circle, caught her attention. He demonstrated strength and a good work ethic that she thought added to their chances. When she looked to Tom, she now knew he wouldn't work them to death. She liked controlled work, not work to the point of exhaustion. Right now, she was exhausted.

She ran her eyes up Ashley's long legs and over her down parka to her pleasant face and remembered when she herself might have been as attractive. Even more impressive was her work ethic and thus her value to the collective effort. The swim across the river and climb up the mountain were even more impressive. Sandy enjoyed the opportunities she had to talk with Roberta. She looked forward to completing some of those conversations. For tonight, she simply wanted to go to bed and think about preparing the fish for Tom in the morning. She kept Tom's earlier talk with her safely tucked away. It helped.

Paul stared into the flames and tried to envision each of his fellow campers. The newcomers, Eric and Connor, didn't offer much intellectually. If they pulled their weight, Paul thought he could ignore them. They presented an enigma for Paul. His restaurant catered to rich people with varying personalities. Some of his rich customers were socially committed, perhaps in the mold of JFK or George H.W. Bush, willing to put their lives on the line when duty called. Other rich customers came from Trump's Cadet Bone Spurs camp. When push came to shove, he wondered where Eric and Connor would line up.

He appreciated how Ben had negotiated with Tom to take control. Ben made the group effort more cohesive and therefore stronger. Paul knew he would have to live with his initial feelings about Tom. He also knew that his momentary lapse in human decency would strengthen his resolve to help Tom any way he could.

He'd had a few discussions with Jerry and Roberta in the days before the earthquake and found them agreeable. He thought they were good people and he was glad they were on the trip with him. He viewed Jerry as a well-refined professional with military clearances. Jerry didn't talk about his job but was always pleasant and comfortable to be around. Roberta showed a more open personality with a willingness to ask pointed questions. Paul wondered if he interpreted Roberta's personality correctly, since his minimal interactions with her indicated significant divergence from Jerry's congenial personality. Where Jerry would avoid a challenging question; Roberta seemed to have a more demanding demeanor.

Walt held a special niche in Paul's thoughts about survival. The way he pitched in and worked hand in hand with Ashley to help Tom impressed him. He hoped nobody needed additional medical help, but he knew dedicated skill would be available if it were needed. And Rick could do some heavy lifting when required.

Paul appreciated the responsibility Tom bestowed on him and Sandy for nutrition. He knew he wouldn't fail the group. Paul's tour as a rock band manager landed him in the San Francisco Bay Area several times. He always relished his time there. He intended to talk with Ashley about some of his favorite haunts. Maybe he would bring up some memories from the bayside bars in Sausalito, or some of the colorful venues on Broadway. But most importantly, he wanted to talk to her about her trek up the mountainside. He thought talking about it would be a great way to thank her, along with actually thanking her.

Aside from Tom's knowledge and skills that gave them a chance of survival, Paul wondered about him. Tom had a positive strong presence; that didn't just happen. Paul thought there must be something more behind that battered body. He admired Tom's tenacious strength.

Rick rested his elbows on his knees and held his chin in his hands. Without moving his head, he shifted his eyes just enough to see each of the campers. Rick gladly worked for and with the group, but he didn't feel comfortable trying to be an actual participant in anything other than work. His companions outclassed him intellectually and financially. He didn't want to be caught staring at any of them. Rick didn't dislike any of them; in fact, he would welcome opportunities to talk to each of them. For now, he would simply keep his place.

Tom had replaced Branch as the wilderness expert. No skills were lost in the exchange. Tom's demeanor didn't mirror Branch's perpetual people skills, but the circumstances had changed such that it didn't matter. What Rick had intended to learn from Branch he could just as well learn from Tom.

Rick caught a glimpse of Eric and thought he and his brother were unrealistic when they came upon them, as did the rest of the group. He assumed they commanded wealth and that they went through life as it pleased them. He wondered what he would do with that kind of money.

His focus shifted to Ashley. Good job, good looking, and smart. Everything he would want one of the partiers at school to grow into. He questioned why she came on the trip alone. It didn't matter; she carried her own pack and kept up. Her courage impressed him because she didn't hesitate to work in the blood to repair Tom. Last night's heroics put her in a special class.

Paul and Sandy represented exactly what Jim had told Rick to expect on this trip. Successful people with pleasant personalities. People that could afford the trip. He considered the restaurant business a tame endeavor and discounted it as a possible career path.

Jerry and Roberta gave him the impression that they were more interesting. Their comfort zone was obvious. Jerry worked on important projects with military clearances. They seemed exciting. Roberta commanded the power of the pen. Rick thought she had influence because her thoughts were read by millions. The ability to persuade people interested Rick.

Ben's calm and confident manner represented a strong man with character. Rick was impressed when Ben negotiated a plan with Tom. When he volunteered to cross the river and climb the mountain in the dark, he earned a special kind of respect.

Walt had taken an interest in Rick before the earthquake. Rick liked Walt's easygoing manner and his willingness to help him around camp.

Of all the campers, Rick decided he could interact most easily with Walt.

As was Jerry's custom, he had quietly assessed all the players and intended to keep his thoughts to himself. He surveyed the body postures around the fire. He had already observed their work ethic, conversations, and demeanor on the trail. Now he consciously connected what their bodies were telling him. He looked for discrepancies from what he thought he knew. As expected, Rick sat quietly, slightly hunched over, holding his head in his hands. He avoided eye contact or any other contact. He didn't want to be there, not from exhaustion or hunger, but from a position of unequal status.

Like Rick, Paul stared into the flames. Unlike Rick, he sat up straight, his hands comfortably in his coat pockets. He didn't try to hide his face. He presented an open appearance, available, and interested. He believed Paul was sincere in his regret regarding his comments about Tom. That brief interlude didn't fit him. Paul presented value to the survival efforts, not only in his knowledge of food and nutrition, but as a steadying and unifying force. He trusted Paul to make every effort to promote the effectiveness of the group without self-serving or selfish motives. A good choice for control of the food.

Sandy's current body language didn't conform to what Jerry expected. His conversations with her led him to believe that she fit perfectly with her husband: socially adept, physically fit, and confident, at least prior to the earthquake. Her darting eyes and slumped shoulders now hinted at something else. Perhaps fear had entered the equation. Maybe she wasn't as strong as he had assumed. He would wait, and not pass judgment. Perhaps she simply needed a good night's sleep. In any event, Jerry assumed she would work alongside Paul in their wilderness kitchen.

Eric and Connor were just there. Physically, they were neither robust nor weak. Their physical participation, since they accepted the loss of their moose head, was more than acceptable. Their social interactions left a lot to be desired. They kept to themselves as much as possible. Jerry didn't know whether they actively disliked anybody, or if they simply detested their predicament in general. Jerry assumed they had never done anything important in their lives. The question remained. Was there an inner strength in them that had never been tested? For now, if his life depended on some help, he would look elsewhere.

Jerry took note of how Walt always willingly made himself available to help anybody with any minor task. Walt remained quiet but seemed able to maintain a smile and provide encouragement for his friends on the trek down the river. Thoughts of Walt brought forth a saying Jerry's father had used: "If you need a job done, give it to a busy man."

Ben sat up straight with his shoulders back. His eyes confidently scanned the circle. Jerry had talked with him several times prior to the loss of their leaders and respected his common-sense approach to life. Ben exuded strength, confidence, and stability. Jerry knew that if things got completely out of control for the group, Ben would be the last one to panic. It was as if Ben had seen tough times, survived them, and knew the only way out was forward. He intended to stay close to Ben.

Ashley's presence at the fire circle fit Jerry's previous impressions just as well as the fit he had formulated for Ben. She was a woman of confidence, inner strength, and commitment. Jerry and Roberta had talked to her on the first day of the trip. They found her open and interesting. They were impressed with how Ashley articulated the way the landscapes and openness of Alaska reminded her of her childhood. She emphasized how welcome it was, compared to the corporate confines she worked in. Jerry studied her presence at length. She sat confidently, comfortably, and fearlessly. She wasn't afraid of the wilderness, the situation, or anybody at the fire.

Finally, Jerry focused on Tom. There was a young man working and living far beyond his age. Knowledgeable. Confident. Competent. Strong. All the above fit Tom. Jerry wanted to know more about him. This package couldn't just happen during his relatively short life in the wilderness. Somehow Tom had developed a foundation for his life. Were his parents that good? Did he read? What did he read? What and who was responsible for shaping this superhuman? Jerry shook his head slowly, acknowledging his admiration for Tom.

Roberta assessed the personalities and convictions of people around the fire. Rick proved an easy read. He sat at the fireside and tried to disappear, though not from fear or disdain. He worked hard for the group and everybody liked him, but his youth and insecurity worked against him. Ashley was almost the opposite. She stood out. Even in silence she commanded a position in negotiations and decisions. Her commitment to the group was well established.

Conversations with Paul and Sandy convinced Roberta that their civility guided their lives. Even here in dire straits, they made every effort to maintain an air of social correctness. Roberta thought she could depend on them to float the group to maintain high standards. She hoped together they could keep the group from sinking into depression or base thoughts and language.

Walt's personality matched his work ethic. He continually strove to help wherever he could, never with a loud or critical word. Roberta wanted to help him keep the group cohesive and forward looking. Then Roberta considered Ben. Not only physical and handsome, but the silent strength of the group. He didn't waste time, motion, or speech. When he worked, it was with attention to detail. When he spoke, he had something to say. No surprise he managed to consolidate the group behind Tom, and just as likely that he made the trek with Ashley. If necessary, she would lean on Ben.

Eric and Connor were just there. They worked; in fact, they worked hard. She thought if they worked and otherwise stayed out of the way, it would be just fine.

Tom was in charge. Roberta knew there had to be something more to Tom than a simple wilderness man. Although he made every attempt to close himself off, he was open-minded and sensitive to the needs of the group. Something told her he had the makings of a worldly figure.

Ashley quietly observed the circle of individuals united in a common cause. There was no reason to suspect anybody had less than a full commitment to a community effort. She found herself able to talk to any of them and enjoyed talking to most. Survival was less than a certainty, but she relished the adventure. The stark landscapes reminded her of her childhood home. Unfortunately, she couldn't go back there, so she enjoyed the similarities. Ashley possessed some expertise that might help, and she recognized other capabilities within the group. The trekkers' dependence on Tom wasn't worthy of a notion. It was absolute. She thought the best chance for survival would be to maintain a coordinated congenial work ethic.

Ben accepted the group as it was. He would play the cards as they were dealt. There were no favorites, and certainly no enemies. He found encouragement in that everybody worked for the group without hesitation or complaint. He knew that held the key to survival.

Tom surveyed his responsibilities. He searched each camper for individual needs. Fear, physical problems, and depression, if left unattended, would weaken the group effort. Rick's physical posture at the fire would have concerned Tom if he hadn't talked with him enough to understand that he was okay. Sandy gave him encouragement. He thought their talk helped reassure her. Eric and Connor were aloof, but they demonstrated good work ethics. He hoped that would continue. Ashley would do anything necessary, and along with Jerry, Ben, and Walt, she was one of the four people Tom knew he could depend upon if needed.

Tom's only concern centered on total fitness for survival. That fitness comprised both physical and mental toughness. His inherited dependents were willing workers and they agreed to sacrifice personal comfort for the group good, but Tom worried about how far he could stretch those attributes. What was the breaking point? When would good intentions descend into inaction, depression, or worse—panic? Survival in these conditions depended on a total package. Except for the brothers and Rick, whom he thought he could train, everybody had demonstrated the toughness required to excel in their chosen professions. He hoped that toughness could be transferred to survival here in the wilderness. He expected that the success of Ashley's action plan would provide a model for them to follow.

Walt held his place at the fire. His reticence and quiet nature contradicted his value to the group. He searched for chinks in the armor all the campers tried to shield themselves with—not in preparation for his attack, but for someone he could prop up, support, or defend. Ben could have explained Walt's thoughts. Nobody else would ever have guessed.

Walt thought back to his first experience with psychological help and how it affected his life. In a large high school in Southern California, Walt and some friends had permission to form a container-plant-growing club. In preparation for their first meeting, Walt's friend Betty had drawn pictures of several flowers on the meeting room chalkboard. A half-dozen friends talked casually before they called the organizing meeting to order. A noisy bunch of boys from the football team stood outside the door and made rude comments. Walt walked toward the door to close it but before he reached it, four of the noisy boys entered the room and told the potential club members they needed the room for themselves. Walt protested and they pushed him aside as they made their way to the chalkboard. They crowded Betty out of the way and began to defile her artwork. Walt and another boy protested loudly. The intruders shouted at them and told them to leave if they didn't like it.

Then, something happened that Walt still marvels at. A large boy, who appeared to be Middle Eastern, stood in the doorway. He had been in the hallway and observed the problem. His voice was deep and soft. "What's the problem here?" he asked without agitation.

The boys at the chalkboard said there was no problem.

The boy in the doorway said, "There must be, because you're disrupting their meeting."

Another hefty boy took a step toward the doorway and said if he didn't like it, he could leave.

The calm boy in the doorway said, "No, I think you should leave."

The noisy boy said, "No, geep, I'll help you leave," and started toward the calm boy, who met him halfway. In a show of strength and quickness, the calm boy grabbed the intruder by his shirt with one hand and his belt with the other, picked him up, and threw him through the door and into the hall. The intruder skidded across the hallway floor and found himself crumpled against the lockers on the opposite wall. Then the calm boy approached the boy at the front of the room. Without another word, that boy and his companions scurried to the door. Walt asked the calm boy his name; he replied, "Jalib."

The football coach, on hall duty, came to the door after he watched one of his players exit the room awkwardly, followed by three more. The coach asked Jalib if he ever played football. No, he answered. The coach asked if he wanted to play. Jalib said no. The coach said that was too bad. After looking around, he said it looked like everything there was okay. Walt thanked Jalib and asked if he was there to join the club. He said no and left the room.

Walt wanted to be Jalib's friend. He searched the halls for almost a week before he saw him with Karen, a good student with blond hair. Walt didn't interrupt them. The next day, Walt found Karen alone and asked about Jalib. Walt asked if they were friends.

Karen answered, "I wish. He said it wasn't a good idea for me to be seen with him." Walt asked why. Karen said Jalib just said it could never work out. She began to cry and walked away. A week later, Walt asked Karen about Jalib again. She said he moved away.

Walt always hoped that boy found friends and happiness; he deserved it. The willingness of that boy to do the right thing set the course for Walt's life.

CHAPTER 9

A light rain addressed the campers in the morning. After a breakfast with more salmon caviar, they completed Tom's instructions for the smokehouse.

They started a fire in the smokehouse and babied it until it burned briskly. They left a healthy fire in the firebox to heat the rocky chamber before they put the fish in. Tom invited everybody back to the hot bath pond.

"Will the fish add enough food to get us out of here?" Paul asked.

"Not without cutting back on our diets considerably." Tom didn't tell them that the further they got down the river, the less likely it was that they would find much more to eat. Tom pondered the possibility of going back up to the fishing spot to kill the bear. He knew it was dangerous to compete with the bear for fishing rights. He dismissed the idea. It was best to avoid a confrontation between his companions and one or more bears.

"Oh well, it probably won't hurt most of us to lose a little weight," Jerry said.

"We're all going to do that," Tom said.

"Are there any berries around here we could pick?" Rick asked.

"That's a good thought, but we're a little late. There could be a few, but the bears would have taken most of them by now. Besides, I don't want to compete with the bears for them in the brush." Tom liked Rick.

His physical attributes were suitable for heavy work in the wilderness, he worked well with others, and he asked intelligent questions.

"By the way, Paul, be sure everybody gets occasional vitamin C; lemons or limes will work. We're not going to be out here long enough for serious scurvy, but we don't need any early problems we can avoid."

"I'll take care of it. Onions will also help. I'll make sure everybody eats them whether they like them or not." Paul knew more than enough about dietary requirements.

Roberta leaned back against the pond bank and said, "This kind of wilderness is something I can deal with. Especially since Ashley and Ben put the fear of god in those young men."

"It's almost enough to make you quit worrying about tomorrow," Paul said. "Also, Tom, just in case we don't make it out of here, where I could say this better, thank you for helping us and giving us a chance to get out. And I want to apologize for even considering leaving you. That wasn't right and I feel bad about it."

"Don't worry about it. We're going to do this together. I'm not the perfect patient either. The people I live with here in the wilderness practice independence. We try to never depend on anybody but ourselves. It's not community based, and I guess it works to a point out here. You don't hear 'please' and 'thank you' much. Let me try that now. Thank you. I don't know what would have happened to me if you hadn't come along. And add to that, I remember how I walked out on you. That doesn't feel very good either."

"You're a good man, Tom. I don't want to think how any of us would have reacted if we had suffered your losses," Jerry said.

Eric and Connor sat in the hot water quietly without entering the discussion. They both wondered what the full story was. Nobody had talked about it since they joined the group.

Sandy listened and watched the discussion. At first, she was reluctant to join the nude group in the hot tub. Today, she relaxed and leaned back against the bank. She let her mind drift to how a typical day in

Cleveland would unfold. How she started the day and how it ended with a trip to the gym that would include a session in the hot tub and time in the sauna or steam bath. She detailed the day, starting with the chef in early daylight hours to select fresh meat and vegetables. After that she would review customer comments and inspect linens, flatware, glassware, and china. Then she always reviewed any notes from employees, to detect any personnel problems. When the breakfast crew of cooks, servers, and busboys arrived, she greeted them and asked randomly about them and how the job was treating them. When she satisfied herself that the restaurant was ready for the day, she headed for the gym. Later in the day, Paul would go to the restaurant and do the accounting and banking and cover personnel concerns for the evening shift. It was a good life, and the division of responsibilities still allowed her and Paul to spend time together. And that brought her back to the reality of the hot pond. Really, just another day at work.

Sandy graduated from a culinary management school. She learned to pay attention to the little details. Most importantly, she always tried to balance a comfortable atmosphere in her restaurant between "too personal" and "neglect" for the patrons at the tables. Most of her waitstaff had been with her a long time and she trusted them to maintain that critical balance. She compared the restaurant work with her responsibilities here in the wilderness. She considered everything from raw materials to preparation to service to cleanliness, even to presentation. At first she didn't see it, but after efforts to draw distinctions, she realized she was in the same boat. She zeroed in on her talk with Tom. Everything made sense to her now. Her survival in Cleveland depended upon maintaining those standards. Survival here depended on those same efforts. There were no redoes. You either succeeded or you failed.

After a half hour's soak, they rejoined reality. At the campsite, they loaded the smokehouse with fish and went to work collecting firewood. Other small tasks filled time until dinner.

After dinner, Ashley sat at the fire and contemplated an experience at a spa on the Russian River, north of San Francisco. Susan had arranged it for her birthday. Near the river with pleasant hiking trails and clean air, the destination was worth their trip. A restricted diet highlighted the experience: no pastries or baked goods, minimal fat, and no alcohol. At least it was healthy, she thought.

Ashley stretched her arms over her head and maintained her thought processes. Hot tub soaking and mindful stretching exercises invigorated the campers. Midmorning and late evening discussions were designed to keep the participants from focusing on the dietary restrictions. Tents around a secure area, cooking over an open fire, and eating their meals on their laps. It was fun. She thought about the discussion themes: current events, politics, and personal relations. Yes. Ashley knew Susan would have enjoyed this wilderness spa. She smiled and laughed as she made her way to the tent.

Tom suggested that they relax their regimen and get a little extra sleep in the morning. They deserved it, their spirits were good, and he thought he would allow them to consolidate good thoughts.

Tom rose early but allowed himself some extra time before he started the day for the rest of the campers. A clear sky lifted his spirit and he decided to walk around the campsite perimeter. Unbelievable. He blinked twice and focused on a lone caribou grazing two hundred yards downriver. An opportunity they couldn't afford to miss. Tom hurried back to camp and quietly woke Eric. "Can you hit a target at two hundred yards?"

"Of course."

"Get your gun and follow me. Now." Tom led Eric, in his underwear, along a low spot and then inched his way up onto a sandy bank to find the caribou. It was still in range. "We can use that meat if you can make a clean kill." Eric crawled up on the sand dune and took aim. He fired, and the caribou collapsed. Tom asked Eric if he knew how to take care of the meat. Eric told him that was one thing he knew how to do.

"What the hell?" Paul called out.

Sandy sat up and listened. Then she said, "Do you think there's a bear out there? Or are our friends back?"

"Don't know. I'm going out."

Paul met Ben, Jerry, Connor, and Rick by the smoker. They searched for activity. Finally, they spotted Tom returning to camp.

At the smoker, Tom gave them the good news and sent Connor, Jerry, and Rick to help Eric get the meat back to camp. He also told them to save the antlers and keep the hide intact. Eric watched the kill until Connor walked to the caribou, then he came back to his tent and dressed.

Later in the morning, after the field-dressed meat awaited carving, Tom helped Paul and Sandy inspect the heart and liver. Those organs were in good form, from a healthy animal. Then he recommended that everybody get back to the hot pond to do their laundry, especially socks. Nobody should wander out of camp alone or without bear spray. Also, everybody had a responsibility to collect firewood. Campers made their way in turns to the pond to soak and wash. Then Tom gave them an odd order. He told them that when they picked up a piece of firewood, they should squeeze it and twist it, one hand against the other. He also said that when they sat at the fire, they should do the same thing. Finally, he explained that they would be using their bare hands on the oars to paddle the boat and that their hands would need to be tough. They couldn't afford unnecessary blisters.

"What boat?" Jerry asked.

"Yeah, what boat?" Connor repeated.

"I think we'll build one," Ben said.

The campers looked at each other incredulously. Sandy smiled.

Walt worked with Paul and Sandy to carve the caribou meat. They saved every scrap, per Tom's instructions. The small trimmings from the legs and other bony areas would make good jerky.

Late in the afternoon, Tom went to the pond to wash and soak. He found Jerry, Roberta, and Ashley soaking and relaxing. He asked if he could join them. He went to the pond outlet and scrubbed some underwear and socks. He left the laundry to soak and leaned back against the bank with his face and bandaged arm out of the water. Tom asked how anxious they were to get out of the wilderness. Jerry said he was ready.

Ashley said she would never get enough of the natural beauty, wildlife, and spectacular landscapes. The wide-open, expansive high-desert landscapes in northern Nevada seemed to Ashley like they were magnified here in the Alaskan wilderness, especially the quantity and variety of wildlife. The fact that the wildlife didn't appear around every corner was unimportant. The fact that it could be, was enough. Nevada had mule deer, elk, antelope, wolves, mountain lions, wild horses, eagles, and an occasional black bear. Here, elk, wild horses, and antelope were missing, but moose, caribou, brown bears, wolverines, goats, sheep, and fur bearers more than made up the difference. She almost felt at home here.

"You find it beautiful?" Tom asked.

"I'm sure everybody does."

"I don't; I see work. I don't mind the work, but it's just work."

"Haven't you ever seen any beauty in it?" Ashley asked.

Tom closed his eyes and thought about it for several seconds. When he opened his eyes, he said, "Not out here."

"Where, then, and what was it?" Ashley asked. She was curious what Tom found that was more beautiful than this wilderness.

Tom looked at her. He wondered why she would care. He carefully considered his answer. "I was over at a fishing village once, on the ocean. The low fog blended with the ocean and a fishing boat peacefully moved over the water and sent little waves rolling away. I don't know why, but that scene was the most beautiful thing I've ever seen. Maybe the symmetry was intriguing, maybe it was the way the colors blended, maybe the salt air had something to do with it."

"That's fair enough," Roberta said, and she considered how Tom's analysis seemed more like an art connoisseur than a wilderness guide. She was impressed.

Paul and Sandy cooked and served the caribou heart and liver for dinner, and everybody had all they could eat for the second night in a row. Tom had filled the smoker with the fish and some caribou meat and fueled it with small twigs to create the perfect smoky fire.

Jerry and Roberta scheduled lookouts for bears or intruders. Walt and Ashley checked everybody for footcare, blisters, and general well-being. Rick assured campsite needs were met, including plenty of firewood.

After dinner and cleanup, they sat around the fire in good spirits that invited conversation and opportunities to bond. Walt reminded everybody to get their twisting stick to toughen their hands.

"So, . . . Ashley, why is somebody like you out here alone?" Connor asked.

Ashley thought that was a stupid question but replied without commentary. "I'm not alone; I've made some friends on this trip."

"Yeah, well, who are you sleeping with?"

Ben immediately sprang into action. That was the kind of abuse he wouldn't put up with at home. Here, in this situation, it could be devastating. "What's wrong with you? Has the fresh air affected your brains, or have you always been an idiot?" Ben demanded, as he pointed his twisting stick at Connor.

"Thanks Ben, but I can handle this. Who are you sleeping with Connor, your brother?" Ashley grew up on a cattle ranch with cowboys and knew how to handle herself around rough talk and sexual innuendos. At such times, she was reminded of the story of a young female English professor that received an essay from a freshman who thought he would exercise his literary license with a few examples of locker-room language. The professor marked up the work in red with a note: "I grew up on a cattle ranch and we would laugh at anyone that tried to make a point with weak language like that—so fuck you! If you want to learn how to swear like a real cowboy, make an appointment. Otherwise, use proper English."

"When I get back, I'll have plenty of women to sleep with," Connor replied, heatedly.

"I bet they're all your best friends, too. I have one partner when I get back."

"Well, why isn't he here?" Connor couldn't let it go.

"My partner's a woman," Ashley answered matter-of-factly.

"Do you have any real friends, Connor? I bet you just buy the companionship you need," Sandy said.

"We can afford whatever we need," Eric chirped.

"Your money's not doing you much good out here, is it? Even your very expensive leather boots don't serve you as well as our cheap gum boots."

Connor couldn't come up with a reasonable response and instead asked a defensive rhetorical question. "How much longer are we going to be out here?"

Tom worried about this discussion getting out of control, but he thought a little peer pressure might be good for the group, so he let it go.

Walt thought maybe a little macabre humor would end the abusive discussion. "Oh, maybe until the bears eat us, or if the weather changes enough, maybe we'll freeze, or maybe the food will run out and we starve. Whatever comes first." Holding his hands up as if he'd just come up with a great idea, he added, "Or . . . maybe we'll eat each other."

Eric and Connor realized they were outnumbered, and they had to tacitly admit their money wasn't helping them in the wilderness in general or in the current discussion.

"Yeah, even with Tom, I suppose it could come to that," Roberta said.

"Without Tom, it could've been a certainty," Paul said.

"I think even Tom—no, especially Tom—would admit that there are no guarantees out here," Walt said.

That reality ended the animosity, and Tom suggested bedtime.

That night, a storm moved into the area. By daylight, the campsite suffered a cold rain and gusty winds. The tarps and tents flapped in the wind. The main fire continued to burn under a protective tarp and the smokehouse firebox pushed heat and smoke up through the rocks to cure the fish and meat. Nobody in camp was comfortable. Tom asked Ben and Rick to accompany him up the river toward the small tributary to collect some building supplies. There they found the most important thing Tom wanted: a stout twenty-five-foot-long straight timber with a curved-up end. He marveled at finding what he considered a nearly perfect keel for his boat. He stared into the wind with Ben and Rick and shared a plan.

They collected and stacked several smaller long curved branches that they would retrieve later and carried the long timber back to camp, where Tom told people gathered around the fire that he and Ben and Rick were going to warm up. He offered them the same opportunity. The three men retreated and returned naked on their way to the hot pond. The remaining campers thought about that act. They could huddle around the fire in misery, or they could celebrate the weather and dance their way to the comfort of a hot bath. All but Eric and Connor joined the celebration. Attitude is everything in the wilderness. The mood improved considerably in the hot pond, as the cold rain continued to pummel them.

The wind and rain subsided late in the afternoon and Tom organized another crew to retrieve some of the limbs that had been gathered that morning. With the wood stacked neatly near the boat project, the campers found minor tasks to improve the campsite. Firewood, stretching the tarp over the common area, and upgrading the cooking fire rocks all kept minds off the weather. Even though the rain and wind ceased by dinnertime, cold air reminded everybody that they were indeed vulnerable. After cleanup chores, they huddled around the fire, thinking more than talking.

Connor stood and walked to within a few feet of Tom, who was seated at the edge of the fire. Indecisively, Connor stepped forward and stood close to Tom for almost a minute while Tom peered into the fire without acknowledging him. Connor reached into an inner coat pocket and produced a small piece of paper. "This is a check for a million dollars and it's all yours when you get me out of here."

"What about your brother?" Sandy asked.

"Yeah, him too." Connor presented the check to Tom and pressed it into his hand. Tom stared at it, shook his head with a smirk, and stuffed it in the outer pocket of his coat. Connor backed away slowly in an uncertain manner. His body language and the flatness of his voice told the group he hadn't given much thought to his actions. It seemed more an act of desperation than a commitment. Those same thoughts ran through Connor's mind in a murky sort of way.

"There's your boat, Tom," Roberta said.

Tom didn't say a word. He stood, backed away into the darkness, and disappeared. Tom's reaction reinforced Connor's obfuscated state of mind. Within moments, everybody had left the fire except Eric and Connor. Eric remained silent.

Tom worried about Connor's play, not because of the possible validity of the paper crumpled in his pocket, but because it signaled a possible disintegration of community effort. That would put them all at risk. He couldn't let that happen. Perhaps he could talk to the group about it. He'd already committed to getting them all home. A good probability existed that nobody cared about the paper in his pocket. They were socially committed and reasonable. He rejected talk. He wouldn't have wanted to hear about it. Tom decided that action would speak much louder. He'd let the group watch him send Eric and Connor off to work on their own. Then he would spend some quality time with the rest of the group. When the time was right, he would deal with the piece of paper in his pocket.

In the morning, Tom told Eric and Connor to take a sharp knife, get the hair off the caribou hide, and slice the entire hide into a long strip a half inch in width, like what they had done with the moose hide. Eric and Connor left immediately. Tom suggested the remaining campers go to the hot pond. He shared his plan to build a boat and use the tents to make a waterproof bottom, then shape paddles from more wood and work their way downstream.

After a good soak, work began on the boat. Tom laid the keel and planned the construction by testing the placement of the supplemental limbs. After carefully calculating what else he would need, he sent Ben, Walt, Rick, Paul, and Jerry back up the river to fetch the materials. In addition to the rest of the previously stacked pieces, he also wanted bark stripped from saplings. He would use the strips of bark to lash the wood pieces together and to reinforce the bottom by weaving it forth and back.

Tom had built small boats, similar but much smaller than his current project, to serve minor issues. Those boats were experimental or more like toys, but they were good boyhood projects. Now, that knowledge was critical. One of his boats had been the result of a challenge by his father—build a boat light enough for Tom to carry by himself. He accomplished that with a canoe-shaped vessel he covered with water-proof tarps. He hoped the lightweight tents would serve the same pur-pose. Projects like that filled Tom's childhood and replaced the plastic toys most of the world played with. Practical, original, and intellectually challenging pursuits had served Tom well. This boat had to be light enough for his crew to lift in and out of the water, yet sturdy enough to support eleven adults plus food and equipment. He began the intricate work of fitting pieces by shaping them with the hatchet and his long knife.

When Eric and Connor returned with the rawhide strip, Tom inspected the work and told them he thought it would work.

"Any sign of more caribou out there?" Tom asked.

"Didn't see anything."

"How'd you like to go back down there to see if you can get another one?"

"We could do that."

"Go ahead. Watch for those idiots as well."

Tom began to lash the boat pieces in place. He had the bow and stern posts attached along with a few other structural midsection ribs by the time Ben's work party returned with the requested materials. Tom took time to inspect the size and condition of the pieces, and he put some of them in place to test them further. He told the group everything was looking like it would work.

Eric and Connor backtracked the trail of the caribou they had killed for miles. By late in the afternoon, they were sure the caribou had wandered into the area alone. They returned to the fire just before dark and gave Tom the bad news.

The weather turned agreeable and everybody had a good sleep. First thing in the morning, Tom checked the meat in the smoker. Everything looked good. He bit into a slice of caribou jerky and said it should be packed securely; it would be their last meal. He told Paul and Sandy how to pack the fish and that they would eat it sparingly every day. Then he told them how to slice up the fresh meat and place it in the smoker. He wanted a hot fire in the smoker from that time on.

Tom selected Ben, Walt, Jerry, and Rick to work with him to secure the rails and ribs on their boat. He fitted removable floorboards in the bottom. Floorboards to protect the fabric, removable for weight when they would have to lift the boat in and out of the water. To Tom, it seemed like a perfectly reasonable endeavor to mark each plank to positively identify its appropriate position. Ben thought to himself that Tom thoroughly thought out every action. Likewise, Tom fitted removeable seats. He reminded everybody to help Paul and Sandy process the meat, clean up the camp, and then take some time off.

By dinnertime, the campers had a boat skeleton on the gravel bar. All it needed was a skin. That would happen tomorrow, along with testing and a shakedown cruise. The campers inspected it and were pleased. It was stout and sturdy. It gave them comfort. After dinner, the sky was clear, and a full moon rose over the river. Tom said he was going to the hot pond.

The time in the pond was the most calming time any of them had experienced since the earthquake. At least for the present time, they had food, a hot bath, clean clothes, a boat, and a full moon. The one constant thought for all of them was the fact that they had a competent leader.

"You know, Tom, I studied management styles and leadership in my MBA program, and I've spent my life in the corporate world, but I've never seen anybody put the theories to work like you have," Jerry said.

"I've never studied anything like that. My education is what I could get at school during the winters we spent in town." Then Tom added, "If you knew what you should do, why weren't you taking control when I met you?"

Jerry took what Tom said as seriously as if Tom had issued a life-or-death order. He thought about it a while before he answered.

"I . . . I don't know. There seems to be a chasm between knowing and doing. I suppose it's revealing that I'm an assistant vice president instead of an executive vice president. If I had taken charge, there's a good chance I'd have made some bad decisions." Then after more thought, "No, you're right. I should have done more. In fact, I should take more control at work as well."

"You take orders well, and you're a good worker. I think everybody should do that before they're ready to take over. And besides, show me somebody that never makes a mistake and I'll show you somebody that's not doing enough."

"Living proof; we don't need an expensive university degree to get an education, whether it's leadership or wilderness survival," Ashley said.

"We're about to leave and get down the river soon. But I'm going to miss our wilderness spa," Ben said.

"That's a perfect way to describe what I've been thinking—our wilderness spa," Ashley repeated.

"The rest of the world is still spinning, but we've got our own little microcosm, right here," Sandy said.

"People are people, whether we look on the macro side in the great big world or our own little group. We've all got prejudices, aspirations, and dreams. And sometimes, unfortunately, greed, fear, and animosity enter the picture," Roberta said.

"Circumstance puts a little different emphasis on those ingredients," Jerry said.

"Nothing like a little fear to bring people together," Paul said.

"Or to bring some neurons in our brains to activity that we've been trying to keep hidden; lies, truths, and memories we'd just as soon not face," Roberta said.

No one responded or bothered to ask Roberta for some clarification of her nebulous statement.

"The emphasis might be the same, just different circumstances," Ben said. "Fear does bring people together. Like here in the wilderness, or you can consider how the world came together over the fear of Communist Russia's nuclear threat during the Cuban missile crisis. There are times when fear is deserved. Too often it's just the first thing we jump to," Ben said.

"Yeah, and that's the real social tragedy of the human experience. Will we ever learn to set aside greed, lust, and prejudices without first being fearful?" Roberta asked.

"Fear is nature's first survival tool. It's built into the base of our brain. When fear arrives, we automatically go into fight-or-flight mode," Jerry said.

"But I would argue that if we're aware of the way our brains are wired, we should be able to redirect those fear responses. Be aware. Is your brain's primal interpretation of danger real or imagined? If it's only imagined—get over it. In other words, if we fear people simply because they don't look or sound like us, why act on it?" Roberta said.

"It depends. Out here you don't have a lot of time to react to a noise in the bushes," Tom said.

"Circumstances matter," Paul said.

"Circumstances or situations matter, but even out here a noise in the bushes has to be considered. That noise could be a mother bear preparing to protect her babies, or it could be your next meal. You can't afford to run away from every noise," Jerry said.

"I guess that's true. Even out here, everything must be considered," Tom said.

"A noise in the bush matters. Words matter. Options matter," Roberta said.

"Options?" Rick asked.

"Yes, options. We've always got options. The world is full of options. Consider the options and make a decision."

"You think we've always got options?" Sandy asked.

"Of course. Like Tom pointed out, sometimes we don't have a lot of time to consider them. But they're still available."

"I guess that's true. Just because we don't like any of the options, doesn't mean they're not available," Ashley said.

"Sometimes you have to go with your first impression, sometimes you have to make calculations," Jerry said.

Roberta said, "There's a process. Benjamin Franklin introduced us to the 'T.' Basically, he taught us to divide a paper in half by drawing a line down the middle. Then he advised that we write down all the good things on the left, pro arguments. On the right, write down all the con arguments. Don't live with the initial list. Use the time you have effectively. Sleep on it. Then review the list. Often new items on both sides come to mind. Old Ben didn't stop there. He also told us how to analyze the options. Calculate the probabilities and consider the best and worst possibilities for each option."

"Sometimes you don't have a pencil and paper available," Rick said.

"Once you practice the discipline enough, you can make the basic decisions in your head," Jerry said.

"How do you calculate probabilities?" Tom asked.

"Sometimes it's obvious. If you flip a coin, the probability is 50 percent for a head to come up, one half, one result from two chances, one divided by two. Sometimes experience must give you some guidance. For instance, your calculation of the probability that the bear could be scared away from the fishing hole with just your voice was probably high, maybe 80 percent. On top of that, if we didn't scare him away with our voices, you might have calculated that there was a 50 percent chance that a gunshot would scare him away. Beyond that, if the noise didn't scare him away, you figured there was a 95 percent chance that we could kill him with the gun. That's the first step. Break the problem down and assign initial probabilities. Okay?"

"Yeah, I might change those probabilities. I can see that, but there must be more. How do you arrive at one answer?"

"You combine those probabilities like this. If our voices didn't scare him away, there was a 20 percent (100 percent minus 80 percent) chance we would have to resort to a warning shot. In other words, there was a 20 percent chance that our voices alone would fail. And if we failed, we would take the next step, fire a warning shot. There was a 50 percent chance that would work. Therefore, we had a 50 percent chance of failure. 50 percent of 20 percent equals 10 percent. Now our failure rate is 10 percent. And if a warning shot didn't work, our last resort was to kill him. If we had to try to kill him, there was a 95 percent chance of success. Therefore, there was a 5 percent chance of failure. Before trying to kill him, our failure rate was 10 percent, multiplying that by the probability of not killing him with the gun, 5 percent yields .5 percent.

There was a .5 percent chance the bear could have killed us. You can put whatever percentages you want on the problem, but the process is solid."

"Yeah, I see. Experience helps a lot. But I didn't have to figure all the numbers. All I knew was that we had a very good chance of success."

"Your mind is an amazing thing. Your brain did it for you. Everybody does it all the time."

"But how did Tom's brain know what numbers to use?" Sandy asked.

"Tom has watched bears and remembered how they react. Other people have told him about bears. He knows how effective Eric's gun is. After that, it's just the magic of chemicals in his head that put it all together," Ashley answered.

"It's almost beyond comprehension when you try to think about it," Paul said.

"From what you've said, I see that breaking the problem down into small parts is the starting point," Tom said.

Jerry marveled at how Tom grasped the critical points from a previously unknown discipline. "Ashley, you must calculate probabilities with your computers."

"Yeah, but I only have to frame the right questions. I've got a lot of computing power to calculate the answers."

"Ah yes. Framing the questions is critical," Roberta said. "You can't fully understand your options without asking the right questions. And like Tom said, breaking it down into smaller and smaller pieces until you have easy questions. Sometimes when you break it into small enough pieces, you discover that you already know the answers."

"Just assemble the pieces and calculate?" Rick asked.

"It seems to me," Tom said, "that you can't stop with your first set of pieces or options. Sometimes new pieces appear from almost nowhere. If you look at a problem from a different perspective or have somebody else look at it with a new set of eyes, new ideas can emerge. Climb a tree, dive to the bottom of the river, look at it from a distance, or just sleep on it, like you said."

"What if you don't have any way to know the probabilities? Sandy asked.

"Then you either have to guess at a range of probabilities, or what often seems like a good way to estimate is to get a number from as many people as possible and average them," Jerry said.

"You just guess?" Sandy asked.

"Yes. Just make three guesses, say 30 percent, 50 percent, and 70 percent. Then, do all the other calculations three times, once for each guess. You won't know which one is close to correct, but you will have an accurate range of possibilities. Try it for yourself. After our voices failed to scare the bear away. Insert 30 percent, 50 percent, and 70 percent for our initial value of 50 percent, the chance of the gun-blast sound scaring him away. Then complete the equation with the failure rate of not killing him."

"Okay. Why ask as many people as possible if they don't know any more than you?" Rick asked.

"Statistically, the average of a large number of estimates is more accurate than a single guess, even from a so-called expert," Jerry said.

"I'd like to know more about probabilities," Paul said.

"I'd like to know more about how our brains work," Ashley said.

Eric and Connor remained on the periphery, but they listened to everything. They paid attention and took mental notes as if they were back in a classroom.

After a civilized time in the pond, the campers made their way to tents and sleeping bags. Ashley crawled in and seriously considered the technical aspects of options, decision making, and probabilities. She let her mind wander through the methods and tools she used for her own decision-making. Ashley realized she knew more about how a computer worked than how her brain worked. She could frame a question, enter data, press a button, and expect an answer from her computer.

She could trace the flow of electrons through electrical contacts, resistors, hard drives, displays, and printers. She knew how each bit of every byte of data would be used, where it would be stored, the sequence of use, how the electrons would be recalled, added, stored, recalled, and printed. She had written the programs to control that very flow. All straightforward, no mystery; it was a perfect mechanical system.

Then her brain went fuzzy. How would her brain process the same kind of information? Eyes and ears recognize input sources and somehow convert it . . . to what? Something happens in that mushy mass that lives in the skull. Then she remembered Roberta's admonition: break it down into small pieces. That's fine. Which pieces? What are the pieces? Neurons in the brain are activated with electrical impulses initiated by chemical changes. Release a chemical, stimulate an electrical impulse, and activate another neuron. Easy, right? Which dendrite releases how much chemical and how many neurons are involved to store the numeral five? Does the numeral five always get stored in the same neuron or mass of neurons? What if you need to store a second numeral five? Does it open a second neuron or mass of neurons? Or does the system have a specific area for the numeral five with an indexing system of neurons identifying five(a), five(b), et cetera? It works, she thought.

Then Ashley attempted to conjure the chemicals and electrical impulses required to give Tom the confidence required to challenge the bear and his fishing rights. Her brain spewed forth the components: I want to fish, I want you to leave, there's a good chance we can chase you away with our voices, if not we'll warn you, if not we'll kill you, I know your habits, the probabilities are X, Y, Z, I know how tough you are, I know the power of the gun. How could Tom's brain direct and redirect enough chemicals to arrive at an answer? She knew she could write a computer program to calculate an answer in less than an hour. Tom's brain did it in seconds, or parts of a second. Ashley went to sleep totally unimpressed with modern technology, and with a commitment to studying the brain, perhaps even going back to school to study neuroscience.

Eric and Connor laid in their sleeping bags and did the calculations. They used the probabilities given and talked out the calculations for each of the three options. Then they assigned values they assumed each of the campers might give for the effectiveness of the gun and its ability to kill the bear. Numbers ranged from 80 percent for Sandy to 100 percent for themselves and Tom. They amazed themselves to see how close the average came to 95 percent.

Everybody slept well and woke to a morning damp with a heavy overcast, but no wind or rain. Tom told them it was time to consolidate the use of the tents. He selected three tents he wanted to use as a skin on the boat. He warned them he may need another one or two, but he wanted to start with three. Ashley moved her tent's contents to Paul and Sandy's tent. Rick gave up his tent and moved in with Ben and Walt. Eric moved in with Connor. Tom wanted all tent repair kits collected and delivered to the work area. He and his crew began positioning, stretching, and tying the waterproof tents onto the skeleton. By early afternoon, they had the seams rolled together, tied, and glued where necessary. The excess tent strings provided necessary lines for the boat. Tom worked on shaping paddles from the remaining wood.

Finally, it was time for a maiden voyage. Tom selected Ben, Walt, Jerry, and Rick, the heaviest campers, to help launch the boat and join him in testing. Tom cautioned the crew about the importance of protecting the fragile tent fabric from gravel and sand. They couldn't run the bow up onto the beach for boarding operations.

He attached the caribou antlers to the bow of the boat. Tom's artistic yet practical touch made everybody smile. The lower part of the hard antlers would protect the bow from minor incidental collisions underwater, while the antlers above the water line added a Viking touch. The barefooted crew carried the boat into shallow water. The boat floated.

Tom showed the crew how to lift each member up and into the boat and explained how they would pull the last member into the boat. With that knowledge, Rick lifted Tom up and into the boat. Tom moved about the boat; it seemed stable. He sat on the gunwale—the upper edge of the boat—without any significant chance of capsizing. Tom sat on the far side and asked Rick to lift Jerry into the boat. Jerry joined Tom on the far side of the boat and still the boat remained stable. Tom said he was pleased. The rest of the crew climbed onboard. Tom took his position in the stern with a steering paddle and the crew began to paddle. A half hour of testing proved they had a boat that improved their odds of getting down the river.

The inverted boat on the gravel bank made an acceptable substitute for the missing tents. Tom checked the meat in the smoker and told Paul that it would be ready to pack in the morning. Tom also told Paul to cook the fresh roast for dinner and encourage everybody to enjoy it because it would be their last opportunity to get all the food they would like for a while. The campers filled their plates and complimented Paul and Sandy for a meal as good as they could ever expect. Tom then announced that they would be leaving first thing in the morning and said they might want to enjoy one more soak as the moon came up.

After a good soak they congregated around the fire. Eric and Connor were ecstatic over the status of the boat. They rightfully believed it was their best ticket out of the wilderness.

"We paid our way. We're going to get out of here," Connor said.

"How'd you pay your way any more than the rest of us?" Roberta asked.

"Tom's got his million," Connor answered arrogantly.

This had to stop, Tom thought. He was ready for it. Tom stepped toward the fire and knelt to pick up a burning twig. He stood and held the flame steady as he reached into his pocket and produced Connor's check. He lit the check on fire and held it until the flame closed on his fingers.

"There goes your boat, Tom," Roberta said.

"Even if I thought that was real, it was no ticket to special treatment. If any of us get out of here, we'll all get out together," Tom said, repeating a refrain he had delivered before. He stepped back into the darkness.

"It was real," Eric said.

Tom had been sleeping under a tarp, but now he had legitimate shelter under one end of the boat. Ashley brought her sleeping bag and unrolled it under her tent that was now part of the boat and slept under the opposite end.

CHAPTER 10

A calm night gave way to mist and low clouds before daylight. Paul and Sandy packed the last of the meat with the rest of the food and moved it to the shoreline, ready to load in the boat. Everybody worked together to pack and stack equipment and supplies. Grand smiles and exhilaration buoyed the campers as Tom and Walt worked in the boat to store everything down the centerline. Then Rick helped lift everybody into the boat. The crew pulled Rick into the boat, and they began their boat ride to safety and home.

A light breeze blew down the river and lightly rippled the water. Ashley took a moment to admire the scenery up the river one last time. Late fall colors blazed in the foreground. Behind the bright colors, dark evergreens climbed to the tops of the mountains. In the distance, snow-capped mountains intermittently made appearances between floating clouds. She considered Ben's statement. She too would one day miss their wilderness spa.

The fully loaded boat floated evenly in the river backwater, waiting to be paddled into the current. Walt and Ashley assumed their paddling positions on seat one. Behind them, Sandy and Roberta waited for instructions. Connor and Eric paddled from the center positions, then Jerry and Paul took the fourth row. Tom wanted his strongest and most dependable men, Ben and Rick, with him at the back of the boat.

Walt and Ashley's primary responsibility was to protect the bow from grinding against gravel or other obstacles.

They all paddled in shifts. Rows one, three, and five began paddling and got the boat into the slow current. Tom used his rudder paddle to guide the boat into the most favorable river channels. After fifteen minutes, rows one, three, and five shifted their paddles and rows two and four took a turn.

During the second hour of paddling, Tom wanted to test his crew and the boat. He maneuvered the boat into the center channel and asked all paddlers to give him maximum power. The boat responded well until some paddles got tangled. Odd-sized strokes caused the problem. Tom told them to try again. Again, the boat responded and again some paddles worked in opposition. Tom instructed them to standardize the stroke length and to watch and follow the paddles in front of them; he didn't want to have to sing a cadence. They tried again. The uniform strokes helped, and the boat responded. Cooperation and conformity made a difference. Then they resumed their normal paddling sequence. Tom explained that when he needed full power, it would only be effective when they worked together. Working together was more effective than working as hard as possible with strength only.

After two more hours of paddling, they took a quick lunch break. They tied the boat in a safe position with long lines in protected water. Ashley and Walt took up their responsibilities and checked all hands for blisters and suggested ways of avoiding and protecting against complications. Tom's suggested twisting sticks had proved effective in preventing serious blister problems.

Daylight hours were critical. Tom paid attention to the condition of his crew. They appeared steady and capable, so he let them paddle until almost sunset. It was dangerous to paddle after dark. Grinding the delicate tent skin covering on the boat over an unseen gravel bar was a risk they couldn't take. The danger of a leak was real and would, at a minimum, slow them down. If they lost the boat completely, they would face very real life-and-death decisions. Tom didn't have to explain the details and implications of boat safety. By now, everybody understood and accepted their predicament. Extraordinary care and caution prevailed as they emptied the boat, disassembled the removeable parts, and carried it all safely to the gravel bank. The inverted boat provided a home in lieu of a tent. Security checks, firewood, and a small fire completed the tasks for the day. They finished their sparse meal in the dark without complaint.

"You're getting a little more of this wilderness than you bargained for," Tom said.

"Wilderness is good, if you're prepared for it," Ben said.

"Do you believe you were always prepared for it, Tom?" Walt asked.

"That's an interesting question. I don't think any of us can say we're completely ready for any possible emergency. If you're asking if I felt secure, I would say yes. Do you think you were always protected from emergencies back home?"

"I tried to protect us from other types of emergencies, but I've heard the proposition that all of us are only thirty days from homelessness, starvation, or worse," Paul said.

"My parents and I always had everything we needed out here. I'll admit, though, that I enjoyed the times we spent in Fort Yukon, mainly for social reasons."

"How often did you get to Fort Yukon?" Sandy asked.

"Usually two or three times a year, including the final trip for the winter."

"How long did those trips take?" Walt asked.

"Not long in our jet boat."

"That puts a little different perspective on the wilderness," Jerry said.

"You shouldn't associate wilderness with suffering. We had good clothes, good food, light, and heat. We read. We hunted and fished. We made better than average wages from our gold mine. No, I don't think we suffered. And, we didn't have to live with politics or the economy you have to deal with."

"You make it sound pretty good," Jerry said.

"I wish we had that jet boat now," Connor said.

"That would take all the fun out of this," Tom said.

"You've got a way to make the best of it, Tom," Roberta said.

"Even after you consider all your options, even after you realize you don't like any of those options very much, ya gotta keep smiling," Tom replied.

"I haven't seen much of your smile, but there's no doubt you've got a good attitude," Roberta said.

"Attitude is everything. Everything except sleep, which is something we should get now. Good night."

After a cold breakfast and quick cleanup, they were back on the river for a second day of paddling.

The wide-open stark landscape continued to impress Ashley. She accepted the seriousness of the situation, but that didn't stop her from admiring the wilderness they traveled through. The light, the earth tones, the horizon blending with the sky all reminded her of the sights she admired in her youth. She considered Tom's comments about the wilderness being work. Good work, but always work. Nothing ever came easy. She had worked on the ranch. She had worked hard, but she loved the sights, sounds, and smells of the ranch. She could almost smell the cattle as she considered it.

Paul and Sandy reminded Tom they still had raw meat and wondered how long he thought they could hold it. Tom said they couldn't afford to waste it. He announced that they would stop early enough to cook it and then eat some for breakfast in the dark. Then they would get an early start. They would eat the rest as snacks as they paddled.

That lifted the crew's spirits and boosted the effort they put into paddling. The river depth and width made navigation straightforward and the boat made good progress down the river. Tom identified a likely campsite and they hauled the boat out and left it inverted on the gravel bar. Everybody jumped to the work at hand: collect firewood, get a fire burning, and get the meat on a grill. Paul and Sandy set some caribou strips aside for breakfast. The campers ate caribou ribs with their fingers.

"Well, since nobody has requested dessert, we'll clean this up," Paul said.

That brought some laughs and good smiles.

"There are strange things done in the midnight sun," Tom said.

"'The Cremation of Sam McGee,' by Robert Service. I wish I had my book," Roberta said.

"We don't need a book," Tom said.

"Do you know it?" Ashley asked.

"Sure."

"Please do it; we could use it," Sandy said.

Tom looked around the fire and noticed the eager anticipation on all faces. He smiled. Then, interestingly, he stood and commanded a presence like a well-rehearsed performer. Everyone took note of a Tom they had never seen. He recited the poem slowly in a low and serious tone with emphasis. His delivery caused his audience to deliberate on every word.

> *There are strange things done in the midnight sun*
> *By the men who moil for gold;*
> *The Arctic trails have their secret tales*
> *That would make your blood run cold;*
> *The Northern Lights have seen queer sights,*
> *But the queerest they ever did see*
> *Was that night on the marge of Lake Lebarge*
> *I cremated Sam McGee.*

Now Sam McGee was from Tennessee, where the cotton blooms and blows.
Why he left his home in the South to roam 'round the Pole, God only knows.
He was always cold, but the land of gold seemed to hold him like a spell;
Though he'd often say in his homely way that "he'd sooner live in hell."

On a Christmas Day we were mushing our way over the Dawson trail.
Talk of your cold! through the parka's fold it stabbed like a driven nail.
If our eyes we'd close, then the lashes froze till sometimes we couldn't see;
It wasn't much fun, but the only one to whimper was Sam McGee.

And that very night, as we lay packed tight in our robes beneath the snow,
And the dogs were fed, and the stars o'erhead were dancing heel and toe,
He turned to me, and "Cap," says he, "I'll cash in this trip, I guess;
And if I do, I'm asking that you won't refuse my last request."

Well, he seemed so low that I couldn't say no; then he says with a sort of moan:
"It's the cursèd cold, and it's got right hold till I'm chilled clean through to the bone.
Yet 'tain't being dead—it's my awful dread of the icy grave that pains;

So I want you to swear that, foul or fair, you'll cremate my last remains."

A pal's last need is a thing to heed, so I swore I would not fail;
And we started on at the streak of dawn; but God! he looked ghastly pale.
He crouched on the sleigh, and he raved all day of his home in Tennessee;
And before nightfall a corpse was all that was left of Sam McGee.

There wasn't a breath in that land of death, and I hurried, horror-driven,
With a corpse half hid that I couldn't get rid, because of a promise given;
It was lashed to the sleigh, and it seemed to say: "You may tax your brawn and brains,
But you promised true, and it's up to you to cremate those last remains."

Now a promise made is a debt unpaid, and the trail has its own stern code.
In the days to come, though my lips were dumb, in my heart how I cursed that load.
In the long, long night, by the lone firelight, while the huskies, round in a ring,
Howled out their woes to the homeless snows— O God! how I loathed the thing.

And every day that quiet clay seemed to heavy and heavier grow;
And on I went, though the dogs were spent and the grub was getting low;

The trail was bad, and I felt half mad, but I swore I
would not give in;
And I'd often sing to the hateful thing, and it hear-
kened with a grin.

Till I came to the marge of Lake Lebarge, and a dere-
lict there lay;
It was jammed in the ice, but I saw in a trice it was
called the "Alice May."
And I looked at it, and I thought a bit, and I looked at
my frozen chum;
Then "Here," said I, with a sudden cry, "is my
cre-ma-tor-eum."

Some planks I tore from the cabin floor, and I lit the
boiler fire;
Some coal I found that was lying around, and I heaped
the fuel higher;
The flames just soared, and the furnace roared—such a
blaze you seldom see;
And I burrowed a hole in the glowing coal, and I
stuffed in Sam McGee.

Then I made a hike, for I didn't like to hear him sizzle
so;
And the heavens scowled, and the huskies howled, and
the wind began to blow.
It was icy cold, but the hot sweat rolled down my
cheeks, and I don't know why;
And the greasy smoke in an inky cloak went streaking
down the sky.

I do not know how long in the snow I wrestled with
grisly fear;

But the stars came out and they danced about ere again
I ventured near;
I was sick with dread, but I bravely said: "I'll just take a
peep inside.
I guess he's cooked, and it's time I looked"; ... then the
door I opened wide.

And there sat Sam, looking cool and calm, in the heart
of the furnace roar;
And he wore a smile you could see a mile, and he said:
"Please close that door.
It's fine in here, but I greatly fear you'll let in the cold
and storm—
Since I left Plumtree, down in Tennessee, it's the first
time I've been warm."

There are strange things done in the midnight sun
By the men who moil for gold;
The Arctic trails have their secret tales
That would make your blood run cold;
The Northern Lights have seen queer sights,
But the queerest they ever did see
Was that night on the marge of Lake Lebarge
I cremated Sam McGee.

When Tom finished, everybody had a tension-relieving laugh.

"That's just what I needed," Ben said.

Paul sat in amazement. He'd worked with musicians and performers who knew their way around stages. He couldn't remember any of them with a better presence than Tom had just demonstrated.

"We'll have another good day tomorrow," Tom said. Everybody looked forward to sleep and fulfilling Tom's happy thoughts. Eric and

Connor discussed the performance from their sleeping bags and admitted that perhaps they had misjudged Tom.

They were all tired, but still in stable condition. While all campers slept peacefully, the weather changed, and the weather also peacefully dropped a half inch of snow on the campsite. Cold dry snow greeted the campers when they crawled out at daylight. They dusted the snow off the tents and equipment before any moisture soaked in. The snow didn't do any damage, but the cold and the sight of the snow put a new sense of urgency into the work at hand. All the campers independently beheld the landscape and marveled at the sight of the great white vastness, horizon to horizon. Tom told Eric and Connor to find a high spot and scan the area for game. If there were animals moving, they would be easy to spot. They returned after a half hour, reported no sightings, and helped load the boat.

Again, they carefully carried the boat to the water, loaded equipment, and helped each other aboard. They were underway for the third day on the river. Two hours of relatively easy paddling in the middle of the river made them feel good about leaving their wilderness home. The wide-open, snow-encrusted landscape foretold of the river's course. Against the white land, the dark river water and its course held few secrets. The single main channel divided into several meandering channels segregated by frosted islands. Tom chose a channel and knew they had to be vigilant.

"Ashley and Walt watch the depth of the water. Every time I come down this part of the river, the channels change, and who knows what the earthquake did to it. We'll have to be careful."

"Can't see the bottom here," Walt said. He pushed his paddle straight down into the water without contact. "We've still got a paddle's depth here."

"Good. Keep checking."

Ashley and Walt paid attention to the river immediately in front of them and checked soundings with their paddles. Nobody bothered to bring up Mark Twain stories. Tom steered the boat through the maze of channels that he knew would eventually have shallow water hazards. Then he decided to do some more paddler training. "Okay everybody, let's try something, so we can be ready before we need it. I want you to make this boat go backward. When I give you the command to stop, you hold your paddles flat and still in the water to slow the boat. When the boat slows, we'll paddle backward. We can't let the boat run into something. After we've backed our boat away from a hazard, we might have to get out and guide the boat around. Okay, let's try it. Stop paddling." Everybody stiffened their paddles against the current and the boat slowed. Tom gave the order to paddle backward. The boat continued to slow in the current and then forward progress stopped. The paddlers pushed on their paddles and the boat began to move upstream. "Good job. Let's keep going down the river. Keep in mind, sooner or later that could be important." Walt and Ashley continued to watch for shallow water.

Tom asked whether they needed to stop for a break or if they could carry on making good progress. No reason was given to stop, so Tom suggested they snack on some of the leftover caribou. Sandy distributed morsels and the crew chewed and paddled their way down the river. Early in the afternoon, Walt made a depth sounding and said he found the bottom. He estimated the depth at about three feet. Tom told the paddlers to go easy and paddle slowly and with caution. He scanned the channel options but couldn't identify a channel with any more promise than where he was. They continued to paddle, and Walt continued to check water depth.

"We've got riffles directly ahead," Ashley warned. Tom ordered the boat stopped. All paddlers stiffened their paddles and then paddled backward. The boat moved slowly away from the riffles Ashley had pointed out. Tom assessed the situation and decided to move the boat close to the gravel bank where he could go ashore. He wanted to know exactly how the river looked from a safe position before he risked damaging the boat's fragile skin.

The paddlers maneuvered the boat close to the gravel bar in a backwater out of the current, and Tom stepped off onto the shore. He held the boat and asked Ben and Rick to follow him and hold the boat, so all passengers could exit. They did that, then tied the boat to a large piece of driftwood. For safety, they stretched another rope from the stern to a rock positioned so that the boat would float in water without being able to bounce on the gravel bank. Tom walked down the gravel bar toward the riffles. He stood on the point of dry gravel and concluded that they couldn't take the boat over those riffles. He looked for other options. The paddlers had landed on an island. The river on the other side of the small island moved along a narrow slow-moving channel. Both channels converged where Tom stood. He could see that this would be an easy portage. Beyond the riffles the river looked safe for as far as Tom could see.

Tom went back to the crew and told them what he thought was good news: the river looked safe beyond the riffles. The concept of portaging was foreign to them and the crew thought it looked like work. Nobody complained; it was just something they hadn't anticipated. They unloaded the boat and carried their cargo and removeable boat parts to the point at the end of the island. Then they hauled the boat out and carried it to the water at the last point of gravel beyond the riffles where the two channels merged. They reloaded the boat, climbed in, and continued down the river. Paul asked if there would likely be more portages ahead. Tom said he would be surprised if they didn't find at least a few more. For the remainder of day three on the river, though, they had clear sailing. Tom decided to go ashore with an hour of daylight left. Cooperation created a neat campsite with a fire blazing before dark. Paul and Sandy cooked a preplanned meal and served it as if it came out of their kitchen in Cleveland.

Tom stood and carried his meal halfway around the fire and sat next to Ashley.

"I want to ask why and how you knew how to help me when you found me on the trail."

Ashley smiled and said, "That's two questions. One answer will probably serve both. I grew up on a cattle ranch in northern Nevada. I rode and worked with my dad, my brothers, and other cowboys. Between the horses and haying machinery, we had no shortage of wrecks and injuries. When we got hurt, we patched each other up and went back to the job at hand. It was all in a day's work. So, when you were out on the trail, it just seemed a natural thing to do. Remember, Walt got as bloody as I did."

"I know that. And I appreciate it. How bad was it?"

"You were in trouble; I've seen worse."

"What would hurt you on a cattle ranch?"

That question caught the attention of other campers, and they stopped their private conversations to listen.

"Heavy equipment we used for haying always had danger signs on it. When the hay is ready, you get it done. Sometimes you take shortcuts, drive too fast, and take chances. Things break, and well, it's not a perfect world."

"You handled the equipment?"

"Yeah, from about the age of nine."

"When did you learn to ride a horse?"

"Learn? We just got on—about four, probably."

"You ever fall off?" Connor asked.

"Everybody falls off sooner or later."

"Where do most of the injuries happen, equipment or horses?" Tom asked.

"I don't know. I never kept track. I'll tell you; a cow can do a lot of damage if you're not careful. You always watch out for the bulls. And getting dragged around on rough ground with a boot in a stirrup when you fall off a horse can cause problems."

"Did you ever get hurt out there?" Walt asked.

"I've been patched up a few times."

"Any of them land you in the hospital?"

"I've had a couple broken bones."

"So, working through all that blood doesn't bother you?" Eric asked.

"Nobody likes it. You just do what must be done. Overall, it's beyond just the blood. It's really what all of us are doing now. We just get it done."

"We're glad we've got you on our team. You've done all this before. No wonder it doesn't bother you," Sandy said.

"No, no, I've been in self-sufficiency situations, but this is different; different for all of us, even Tom, I suspect. We're in this for our lives. We don't have any backup. We're it. We either do it or we don't. No, this bothers me—a lot," Ashley said.

"You'd never know it by watching you," Roberta said.

"Looks can be deceiving. I've got a partner that I miss, and she's going to miss me if we don't make it out of here. I guess that gives me some strength to keep putting one foot in front of the other."

"Is your partner as tough as you?" Paul asked.

"Mentally, and smarter."

"Wow, how did you get off the ranch?" Roberta asked.

"School was easy for me. I always found time to do my homework. And I had a few teachers that encouraged me. They used to tell me that I lived in a beautiful place and that they understood it would be easy to just stay put. But then they would say that I should go out into the world and prove that I could excel there too. Being a big fish in a small pond seemed like an excuse to take the easy way out. They said if I could be a success in the big world, I would have more options. And, if I decided to come back, I would have a better perspective on life. They told me something else I didn't appreciate at the time. My favorite teacher said I not only owed it to myself, but to the world. They didn't say it, but looking back, they knew my family life was stifling."

"So, you took the challenge. Was that scary?" Jerry asked.

"I wavered for a while my senior year before I knew I had to try it. An incident on the ranch finally pushed me over the edge."

"Yeah?" Eric asked, waiting for the rest of the story.

"I had tickets to a concert in Reno that I had been looking forward to attending. Those opportunities were few and far between out there. My little brother and I were home alone one weekend. Everyone else had trailered the horses to a cattle camp in the desert. I was taking a bath when my little brother called and said I had to help one of our cows. Well, being raised on the ranch, I jumped into a pair of jeans, pulled on a dirty sweatshirt, and went out to the corral. Just what you'd expect, a first-year heifer was in big trouble trying to calve. Before long, we knew we'd have to perform a C-section on her. I sent my little brother to fetch the medical. I threw a loop and caught her head. Then I tied her to the roping post in the center of the corral. She pulled back on the rope and that allowed me to get another rope to catch her hind legs. I wrapped the rope around a fence post and pulled until she dropped in the dust. I sent my brother, Tommy, for water and we began to operate. I cut her open, saved the calf, and sewed her up. Everybody was happy." Ashley laughed with a half-smile. "I guess I always wondered how she liked the iodine I splashed on the stitches. By then I knew I'd missed my concert and I didn't care. I missed the concert. Then I knew I was going to the big city. I spent a good part of the night back in the tub. If I had decided to stay on the ranch, I never would have a life of my own. My teachers gave me an excuse to leave. I could no longer live my life for the needs of cattle and hay crops."

"Just like that?" Roberta asked.

"Well, a teacher helped me apply to UC Berkeley. They accepted me, and I was off. It only took a few weeks and I knew I'd made the right decision. Academically, I performed well; I found my sexuality; and I never looked back."

"That interests me. The thing about being a big fish in a small pond. I always figured being the best was enough," Tom said.

"It's not a criticism. It's just how the teachers got me to take a chance."

"I wonder how I'd do in Seattle."

"From what I've seen, you'd do just fine. Remember, you don't have to give this up forever," Ashley said.

"Options are always good. Ignorance isn't bliss," Roberta said.

"For everybody?" Connor asked.

"For everybody that thinks. If you have information, you can analyze it. Of course, analysis requires mental gymnastics. Oh . . . I see what you mean. A good part of the population is too lazy to do the analysis work. For them, options are simply a mass of obfuscation. Their favorite saying is, 'Don't confuse me with the facts: I've got a closed mind,'" Roberta answered.

"Do you get back to the ranch very often?" Jerry asked.

"Not anymore," Ashley answered. Then she closed her eyes and shook her head. She thought considerably about saying more. She had shared a nude hot pond and other personal information with people she could die with. She decided to share more.

"No, I'm not welcome there anymore. My father is an elder in an evangelical church and claims he's close enough to god to know what's acceptable in the world, not only for himself, but for everybody else. Looking back, I think he fit Roberta's concept that having facts could confuse him. Too intellectually lazy to consider anything he didn't hear in church. When I took Susan to the ranch, he asked who she was. I told him she was my partner. He immediately and unequivocally said no. He said there was no way she was going to spend the night in his house. Susan said she would take the car and stay in town. I said, like hell. Nobody said another word. We got in the car, bounced out the driveway, and sped down the road. I haven't been back."

"You're a pillar of strength. I'm sorry for that," Sandy said.

"Life goes on. Susan and work are my life now. She asked me several times if I wanted to go back and try to make peace. She reminded me of how her cousin had assaulted us at Thanksgiving. I told her nothing was ever going to change there. It just reminds me; we've got to get out of here."

"How does your mother feel about that?" Jerry asked.

"She died a couple of years ago. At the time, she lived in my father's shadow. She followed him to church, cooked, and cleaned the house. She was never allowed to have an opinion."

"Not exactly a modern-day woman. You've turned the corner about a hundred eighty degrees. You mentioned brothers. Do you ever talk to them?" Sandy asked.

"My younger brother, Tommy, and I were always good buddies and we talk occasionally. I always gave him some protection when things got tense around the house. My older brother followed the image of my father. Tommy says our older brother is drinking quite a bit now."

"Going from cattle to computers is quite a shift in disciplines," Sandy said.

"Just different. The basic lessons I learned on the ranch apply to most aspects of life and work. Show up and get it done. Let's just get it done."

"We'll get everybody home," Tom said.

The fire burned down, and everybody made their way to bed. As usual, Tom and Ashley made space at opposite ends of the inverted boat. Tom twisted uncomfortably in his waterproof tarp. He listened to Ashley breathing uneasily as she twisted and turned in her sleeping bag.

"Ashley," Tom whispered.

"Yes?" Ashley whispered back.

"It's going to be okay. We're getting out of here. I listened to that talk out there, and what you went through with your father had to be as devastating as when I found my mother and father burned in the cabin."

"No, nothing could be as bad as losing a loving family like that."

"Stay strong. We're moving on again tomorrow."

CHAPTER 11

Tom slept on the commitment he'd made. It was now totally personal. He would die before he would let them down. His single-minded determination dominated his every thought. Every action, every pronouncement, every decision would be dedicated to keeping everybody alive. There were no marshmallows in his crew. He maintained a confident stance that burning the check consolidated the group without diminishing efforts from Eric and Connor. Physically, everybody faced the challenges acceptably. After the latest talk around the fire, he considered them mentally tough enough to accept the challenges ahead. For their own good, he would push them a little harder.

When the usual overcast sky first began to lighten, Tom crawled out and started the fire. Without a single rousing wake-up call, his crew dressed and joined him around the fire. Paul and Sandy cooked small portions of oatmeal and served it with small morsels of smoked salmon. They balanced the meal as well as they could. The oatmeal would be filling and provide fiber. The oil in the salmon would provide energy. All campers worked to wash and to clean up supplies and equipment. Eric and Connor worked efficiently and followed Tom's imperatives on their own and by themselves. The rest of the crew interacted and worked together. When the packs lined the bank, Eric, Connor, Ben, and Rick carried the boat to the water and launched it. Fully loaded and with eager paddlers, the boat moved into the current. Rows one, three, and five paddled the first shift. Then rows two and four dug in with equal vigor. Tom found the main channel and guided the boat down the river.

After three hours of paddling through free-flowing water, they floated toward a range of mostly low-lying hills on the left. On the right, the river broadened out into a series of meandering shallow channels.

"I can see the bottom, Tom," Ashley said.

"Stop the boat," Tom ordered.

The paddlers stopped the boat in the channel as Tom had taught them, and Tom inspected the river. His best judgment was that they paddled in the deepest channel available. He needed more information. He ordered the paddlers to move the boat toward the bank on the left.

"Let's unload here and pull the boat out. I need to climb this hill to get a better view." The crew concentrated on their well-practiced routine of unloading, disassembling, and hauling out. With the boat safely inverted on the gravel riverbank, Tom advised everybody to catch a nap if they could. He told Eric to get his rifle and for him and Connor to follow him up the hill. Less than a half hour of climbing provided a perspective on the river. The meandering channels converged back into the main channel about two miles downriver from the hill they stood upon.

"How are you guys doing?" Tom asked.

"We're with you," Connor answered.

"We're doing whatever we can," Eric said.

"Good, we're doing this as a group. What I want you to do is hunt down this series of hills. The rest of us are going to carry the boat up over this hill and down to where the river gets itself together. See that down there?"

"Yeah, I see it. That's going to be a lot of work."

"We'll get it done. Okay. So, you hunt down that hillside, make a circle back and meet us at the base of this hill. If you don't find something out in those hills, pay attention on your way back toward this hill. If there is anything down there, we'll be making enough noise to push it out toward you. Then we'll carry the boat the couple of miles down the river. I figure it'll take us about four hours to get over this hill. Be sure you're here to meet us."

"We'll be here. Hopefully with some meat."

"We'll be listening for a shot."

Tom started back down the hill and the hunters started their quest. Back at the boat, Tom organized tasks. The first order of business dictated that all supplies, boat parts, food, and equipment be transported up and over the hill. They would come back for the boat. Tom wanted the crew to go over the hill to familiarize themselves with the trail and potential hazards before they tried to carry their fragile escape vehicle over the route.

Everybody put on a pack and carried boxes and bags that wouldn't fit into the packs. It appeared that they could carry all supplies and equipment in one trip. They would have to come back for the loose boat parts. Tom led the way. The trail wasn't dangerous, but it was uneven and uphill. Trekking with full packs and carrying boxes and bags took a toll.

"Tom, I'm sorry. I have to stop for a few minutes," Roberta said.

"That's fair enough. Let's take a break. Take the packs off, have some water, and sit down for a rest." Tom knew he had persisted up the hill past the crew's comfort zone. That decision gave him a better feel for the mettle of his charges. Their grit pleased him.

"Tom, have you ever been in a situation like this?" Ben asked.

"What do you mean? I've never guided a group like this before, if that's what you're asking. It's actually a pretty good group. With some proper planning and backup services, we could make something out of it."

"You think we're a good group?"

"I think everybody's come together. Willingness to work is encouraging. We're going to do it. I wondered about you all when we first met. You opened my eyes. I'm actually proud to work with all of you."

"We're glad we've got you too," Paul said.

"That's good to hear," Ben said, "but what I was asking was if you'd ever been forced to face the wilderness with less than adequate tools and supplies."

"My dad and I made some extensive trips by living off the land. If you have a knife and a gun you can usually make a living, depending on the time of year. With salt, sugar, fat, flour, and a few vegetables, you can live pretty well."

After a ten-minute rest, Roberta asked if they could move on. They started up again. A half hour later, they mounted the summit. Tom told them to make their way to the bottom at their own pace. The first one down would come back up to help. Ben, Walt, Rick, and Tom dropped their loads at the bottom of the hill and started back up. When they met each member, they individually took their load and sent them back up the hill. Then they carried the inherited load to the bottom and started back to fetch the boat parts. Well-organized relay teams moved the boat parts up and over the hill. When all loads rested on the down-river side of the hill, everybody made their way back toward the boat.

Tom told Ben, Rick, and Jerry to follow him all the way to the boat. He stationed Paul and Walt a quarter of the way up the hill, and Roberta, Sandy, and Ashley were stationed about halfway up the hill. Despite his still-healing arm, Tom took a position on the boat, Ben, Rick, and Jerry assumed quartered positions, and they started up the hill. A half hour later they met Paul and Walt on the trail. Paul and Walt replaced Jerry and Ben. Tom told them to take a rest and when they were ready, to pass them on the trail and then wait for them further up the hill. They made good progress. With only one rest stop, the boat carriers met the women on the trail waiting to take their turn. Ashley relieved Tom while Sandy and Roberta replaced Rick. Tom and Rick sat on the trail and watched the boat move up the hill. By relaying and mixing the teams the rest of the way up the hill and down the opposite side they caught up to their packs next to the river without damage to the boat. Eric and Connor made their way up the riverbank and met the group within twenty minutes.

"Sorry guys. We didn't even see a fresh track," Eric said.

"It was worth a try. We've got a couple of hours of light. I'd like to get down to the main channel. Can we do it?" Tom asked.

"I'd follow you to the end of the world," Sandy said.

Tom organized relay teams and they made the trek. An hour before dark, some equipment had been delivered to their campsite. Tom relieved Paul and Sandy of their extra load and sent them ahead to set up camp, start a fire, and prepare a prearranged meal. In dim light, they set up tents and finally sat around the fire to eat a welcome meal. Exhausted campers all pitched in to clean up and wash dishes.

"So, uh, Ben. Are you having fun yet?" Walt asked.

Ben laughed out loud. "We'll have some stories to tell when we get back, won't we?"

"What if we don't make it?" Rick asked.

"Life is full of what-ifs. Then we won't have to tell the story. My life has been full and rewarding, especially when I think back to the poor farm my family ran in Alabama."

"Did you have heavy equipment, cattle, and horses like Ashley?" Sandy asked.

Again, Ben laughed out loud. "No, I said it was a poor farm. I remember when my dad was able to retire the family mule and bought an old tired tractor. Everything else was manual labor. He recognized my ability to play ball and gave me everything he could to encourage that. I think I feel worse for my dad—not being able to repay him with a share of a baseball check—than what it could have meant to me. He's a great man. He never complained or even mentioned any disappointment over me not developing into a star player in college. Instead, he made sure he was proud of me for passing the CPA exam."

"Is he still farming?"

"Oh yeah, he loves to make things grow. My career allowed me to buy him a new tractor and some more land. My kids love to go down there and help him drive the tractor. It was worth it."

"Accounting worked out okay, then?" Sandy asked.

"I enjoyed it. It paid well, and I was on track to make partner in another couple of years. That was the good part. But looking back at the situation, I wasn't eating right, and I was drinking with clients more than I liked. I saw clients more than my wife, Annie, and my kids. Annie wanted me to landscape our new home's front yard. I said I didn't have time to do that and hired a contractor to do it. Then I was reintroduced to making things grow."

"Well, that's what happens with landscapes," Roberta said.

"Yeah, but I had forgotten some of the things my dad tried to teach me. When Walt showed up and started asking questions, I didn't have very good answers at first. I asked him about the plants, and he started showing me options. Before long, we went to his parents' nursery and started selecting plants together. Then I found myself in jeans, helping him and getting my hands dirty. One Saturday night after working in the garden, I soaked in the tub and told Annie I thought I might want to find a way to make things grow. She reminded me that my dad was good at it. It's funny how things work out."

"How did it work out?" Sandy asked.

"Walt told me he wanted to expand the family nursery, but his parents didn't need the money and they didn't want the risk or work."

"So, Walt, you were sort of stuck in a hard place, huh?" Jerry asked.

"Yeah, I could've stayed there and worked in the nursery with an occasional landscaping job comfortably for the rest of my life. But I wanted a little more of a challenge. Ben asked if my parents needed me at the nursery. I told him they could hire somebody to do what I did. He asked what it would take to start a first-class nursery. We put it all down on paper and he said he could probably arrange for financing if

I thought we could make a living. I told him we could do it with long hours if we got our hands dirty."

"Ben, you went from clean hands and pencil pushing to dirt under your fingernails," Roberta said.

"Pretty much, and never looked back."

"We learned to share responsibilities. Ben liked it when he had time to get out of the office and help me plant something. When the planting ended, Ben got me involved with the business end of things. There were some long hours and tough times, but our wives joined in and we made it work. If we don't get out of here, they'll never forgive us."

"Did the challenge pay off?" Paul asked.

"I think so. If you buy potted plants in the western US, you probably have some of our work. We have a good landscaping reputation with several subcontractors. We feel pretty good about what we've done," Walt answered.

"How's that working out for your parents?" Roberta asked.

"They're happy as they could be, except they want my wife back. They love her, and they co-opted my kids, and whenever possible, they put them to work in their mom-and-pop nursery. They say they're training them for Ben and me."

"Your wives and kids give you every reason to get back," Rick said.

"Yes, our wives are good friends and they would grieve together. They would be financially secure, but it would take a while for them to get over it," Ben said.

"How about you, Eric, ever make anything grow?" Roberta asked.

Eric looked up, surprised to be asked anything, even with a negative connotation. "No, I never have time for that."

"Might be good for you."

"Maybe."

"Sandy, do you and Paul have any kids?" Roberta asked.

"No. We've both got elderly parents we watch out for. In fact, Paul's mother is going to need special care soon. We don't know if we can put her in a home or whether we'll have to hire a caregiver and bring her into our home. Our only other commitment is to our employees," Sandy answered.

"Eldercare is coming to most of us sooner or later. It's never an easy call," Walt said.

"We don't know what Paul's mother would do without us. She's totally dependent. Both of my parents will need help soon and we don't have any backup. We're both only children, no brothers or sisters and no close cousins. We'll have to make some long-term care decisions before we go on another vacation. Life's so uncertain."

"Don't give up. We're going to do this," Ashley said.

Rick quietly absorbed the conversation. Tom had lost everything. Now he had a self-appointed mission to get everybody out, so they could fulfill their obligations to their relationships. Rick contemplated what he was obligated to achieve. His parents would miss him, so for them, it would be good to stay alive. But still, it seemed to him that he was missing something in his life. The fact that he was still young enough to build relationships didn't console him. Thoughts of his friends at home didn't hold his attention. Parties and dates at school seemed totally superficial. He wondered what those people would think if they could see him here in the wilderness. Would they assume an attitude like Eric and Connor, or would they find a reason to savor life and treasure their friends and fellow travelers? He didn't know.

He tried to honestly assess what his attitude would have been prior to experiencing the current trials. Memories of some beer-induced activities caused him to fear that perhaps he would have been on the wrong side. He knew when he got back, he would have the fortitude to face reality. He also decided that rather than wait until his parents needed help, he would pay more attention to them now. He wondered if Eric and Connor had obligations or whether they cared. He decided that for now, his psychological needs would best be served by helping Tom get everybody home safely.

Ashley looked up into the northern sky and elbowed Ben. "Look at that."

All eyes shifted to follow Ashley's stare. The northern lights had begun to dance across the sky. Red, blue, and green dominated the sky as the sheets of color shimmered and shifted positions.

"That's close to as good as it gets. That's a good one," Tom said.

"Magnificent," Roberta said.

"I'll take that as a good sign," Sandy said.

Paul stared at the show and thought about how he would have photographed it. After running it through his mind, he decided that he was glad he didn't have his camera. Without fumbling with equipment, he could just enjoy it. He could just remember it. And the memory would be as bright as any picture he could have taken.

Ashley lost all consciousness of anything except the sky filled with color. After several minutes, the colors dimmed and assumed a background for the intense memories.

"It's been a long day. Does anybody have any new aches or pains?" Tom asked. Nobody had any complaints, even though they were thoroughly exhausted. "That portage ate into our progress today. I expected to make more miles. I'm looking forward to an easier day. Let's turn in and get some well-deserved rest. I'll see you in the morning."

CHAPTER 12

Tom looked out from under the boat and saw a clear day breaking. Cool, clear air. Just what Tom had hoped for. Everybody suffered a little stiffness from the extended portage over the hill. Tom wanted to get them moving to prevent their muscles from tightening up, but he didn't want to push too hard. They loaded the boat and started paddling. Tom told them not to work too hard. Just keep a steady pace.

That steady pace and a clear course in a stable channel allowed them to make good progress all morning. In the blue sky, tall, steep snow-clad mountains stood out, visible in the far distance. Tom studied the river and possible passages that would maximize their efforts. The water was deep and flowed freely. It was a good day. Tom made occasional searches of the sky for aircraft. He kept his disappointment to himself.

At midday, he gave the order to go ashore for a short break and a snack. The rest of the day proved uneventful. No portages, no shallow water, no complaints. Tom decided to stop early enough to make camp and eat in daylight. He also knew a little extra time off would be good. He wanted everybody to be ready for whatever the next day brought.

Plenty of firewood allowed them the luxury of a bigger-than-usual fire to relax around after dinner and chores. Roberta asked Sandy about Paul's mother and if she lived alone. Sandy said she lived in her own house, but it wouldn't last much longer. Then Sandy asked Roberta if she had any children.

"We have a daughter, a new freshman at the University of Washington."

"I imagine she's been on your mind," Sandy said.

"More than you know. She's a typical teenager, and as such, not ready to be on her own. She's always had options; sometimes she doesn't follow a good one. We're happy she decided to go to school near home."

"How do you feel about that, Jerry?" Sandy asked.

Jerry stretched his arms toward the fire and opened his fists to warm his fingers. He looked at Sandy and said, "I don't think any parent knows for sure when their kids are ready for the real world."

"Jerry, you appear to be easygoing, and from what I've seen, easy to get along with. Roberta, you have some strong opinions," Sandy said.

"Strong opinions aren't bad, though. Everybody likes to be with Roberta. If they don't lie or try to argue by using logical fallacies," Jerry said, still holding his hands near the fire. Jerry's response confirmed what everybody had suspected; that Jerry and Roberta shared a good marriage. Roberta respected Jerry's steady influence and Jerry supported Roberta's activist pen.

Rick stood back a bit from the fire, the warm pockets of his waterproof down parka protecting his hands. "Logical fallacies?" Rick had digested Roberta's positions in previous fireside talks. Even some of her caustic remarks seemed appropriate at the time. He wanted to know more about how she arrived at some of her positions.

"Faults in logic. Presenting an argument based on false or misleading information. Changing the subject without answering the question and answering the question by asking an obtuse question drives me crazy. And talk about crazy. I hate it when somebody tries to generalize an argument from a single case. I'll call anybody out on it every time," Roberta answered crisply as she kicked a burning branch back into the fire.

"What do you mean by generalize from a single case?" Rick asked.

"If I tell you that Medicare is a good thing and you say something stupid like, 'Yeah, well, my neighbor's friend knows somebody that cheats Medicare out of hundreds of dollars. Don't tell me Medicare is good.'There would be two things wrong there." Roberta stared through the darkness into Rick's eyes. "First, don't tell me your neighbor's friend anything. If you don't have names, places, addresses, dates, or something else I can research, don't waste my time. Second, have you ever heard of throwing the baby out with the bath water? If you can identify an incident of abuse, fix it. One cheater should never be an argument for abolishing a good program."

Rick nodded his head as if to say he got it and appreciated the details. "So, you could end some political careers by pointing out some bad arguments," he said.

"I wish. It's not that easy. Connor pointed out the other night that options aren't good for everybody. Not because the options are bad, but because too many people are too lazy to pursue the merits of the options. I say lazy, but it's probably more accurate to say some people don't have the tools to do the analysis. When that's the case, I wish they'd step back and keep quiet instead of promulgating bad information. It's the same with bad arguments. Too many people make excuses for liars, bad logic, and hypocrisy. Unfortunately, many of those same people make excuses for racism too."

"I think we can all agree with that. But that's the world we live in. What do we do about it?" Ashley asked.

"First of all, we never give up the fight," Paul said.

"It's got to go beyond fighting. No, let's not call it fighting. Let's call it our quest for honesty, fairness, and equality," Ben said.

"Being passive about ignorance and racism doesn't seem to be getting us anywhere. Tribalism seems to be a hot term these days too," Sandy said.

"Tribalism is an excuse term. The bottom line: it's truth against lies, decency against racism, education against ignorance, and like we discussed the other night, consideration before fear," Roberta said.

"What do you mean by consideration before fear?" Sandy asked.

"Before we react to anything, we need to better train our brains to have the executive area of the brain override the amygdala—the emotions, and specifically the flight-or-fight area. As we previously discussed, there may well be good reason to fight, but let's consider it first," Roberta answered.

Rick stopped Roberta and asked about the brain, particularly the amygdala. Roberta gave Rick information about how the amygdala is the portion at the base of the brain that is often referred to as reptilian because reptiles' brains operate primarily as the ancient part of the human brain. She explained that the amygdala was responsible for fright and fear as a first response. It is the oldest part of the human brain and the most developed part of the brain in lower life forms. Rick thanked her and continued, "And, of course, fear leads to prejudices."

"There's probably a lot more to it than that. I'm not sure we'll be on the planet long enough for our brains to evolve into peaceful beings."

"What are you talking about?" Paul asked.

"This is my personal thought," Roberta answered, "so, contrary to what I just said I demanded in a discussion, you probably won't find a lot of research material on it. But here it is. Fear is the evil that allowed us to survive when we climbed out of the trees. Friend or foe, I don't know, so I guess I better kill you. The natural continuation of fear is aggression or disappearance. But neither running away nor fighting is what a reasonable person wants to do. Reasonable means the executive function in the brain overrides the amygdala. If the amygdala sent the emotion of fear to the executive function for processing first, before triggering a visceral reaction, the situation could be analyzed. Neither running away nor aggression must result from our first meeting, in the jungle, on the street, or on the floor of the senate. The ancient part of our brain anticipates danger, invokes fear, and causes us to react without consideration. Just because it doesn't look like us or sound like us, doesn't make it dangerous. In other words, put a new twist on Roosevelt's famous quotation, 'The only thing we have to fear is fear itself.' Now wouldn't that be something?" Roberta said.

"What happens when we come face to face with Tom's bear?" Rick asked.

"Circuitry in the brain is pretty fast. We could still run if we had to," Paul said.

"Don't worry. Even if we agree it would be a good thing, brain evolution on that scale would take millions and millions of years. We're not going to be around."

"Sounds like our greatest problem is the attribute that allowed us to survive and evolve in the first place," Tom said.

"I think that's the way it is."

That disappointing fact brought silence and soulful meditation.

"How about something we can do something about. There's a lot of talk about finding a middle ground these days. Is that going to do us any good?" Rick asked.

"Look. If I tell you that the air we breathe is about 78 percent nitrogen and about 21 percent oxygen, I would be telling you the truth. If you disagree and argue that the air is 78 percent oxygen, you would be wrong. Those facts are scientifically provable. There is absolutely no accuracy in your claim. In fact, if your claim were accurate for even a few hours, we would all die. Now, I ask you, why would I compromise the information I know is correct? Why would I corrupt the truth so that I don't hurt your feelings? And that's my real problem. Too many public officials throw out some half-cocked concept and wonder why I won't compromise on what is correct and proper to meet them halfway, even when simple research can prove the point. They won't even read the research materials when I put it in front of them. That's bullshit."

"Why don't you tell him what you really think?" Sandy asked and stuck her elbow into Roberta's side with a smile.

"I could go on."

"Until we can get people to modify their opinions with logic, reason, and compassion instead of emotion, fear, and hate, we're in for a hard ride," Ben said.

"How do we do that?" Ashley asked.

"Options! It has to be options," Roberta answered.

"With no options, you're forced down the same old road," Jerry said.

"Jerry's right. If you've got tunnel vision, you struggle down the tunnel," Paul said.

"Think about Middle America," Roberta continued. "A loud, but small segment of the population is so concerned about staying in a tunnel with a dim light at the end that they will use ridiculous means to keep their friends and family on the straight and narrow. They can't even consider another way to think about the world. The world they've known, the world of their grandparents, is crumbling around them and they're scared to death. I'm reminded of Ashley's home life."

"A segment of that population is scared that their kids will have to compete on a level playing field with kids of color. Racism is alive and well with them. They're afraid that white privilege will no longer be a way of life for them," Paul said.

"That great fear exists in more than Middle America," Ben said.

"Unfortunately, most of them don't even recognize the base root of the problem they're afraid of. Something, something unknown, is changing and disrupting the lives they've always known. I think the educational system is failing to teach people to learn. Yes, facts are good, but the ability and willingness to learn is critical," Jerry said.

"It's more than racism, although a lot of it stems from racism. In order to maintain control, they understand the theory of the big lie," Roberta said.

"What's the big lie? Rick asked.

"If you tell a big enough lie, somebody will believe it. Think about evolution. Some people preach that the world is only five thousand years old. That's ridiculous. We've got living trees older than that—still living. Fossil records, carbon dating, all of science can prove the five-thousand-year-old figure is just not possible. Yet, these people aren't without political power. In at least one state, they have convinced, or coerced, the department of education to remove pages from school textbooks that deal with evolution. If you google some evangelical sites you can find more examples. The sheep simply don't question nonvalidity, regardless of how ignorant the proposition. Their concept of science is something like conjuring the formula for rocket fuel. The scientific method means nothing to them. They simply say 'I'm not a scientist,'" Roberta said.

"Let's go back to your options. How do you empower someone with options?" Sandy asked.

"It's got to be about breaking the cycle of ignorance. Remember, Thomas Jefferson warned us about a democracy and the only way to keep it was to educate the masses. He did something about that. He founded and funded the University of Virginia. Let me give you an example of breaking cycles. It has to do with adult literacy, but I think the lesson is universal. A friend of mine ran a library adult literacy program. He admitted that the effort to teach masses of adults to read didn't result in all the adults learning to read, at least not books. There were some isolated successes, but the true value involved breaking the cycle of illiteracy. He convinced parents that they were not bad just because they couldn't read at acceptable levels. He told them that they survived because they were strong and capable in other ways. They could read the weather, the health of their animals, or the condition of their garden plants. Once the parents believed they had worth in the world, they were able to admit that their children didn't have to suffer the consequences of illiteracy. When reading became important, the children had a chance. He made his point by reciting two hypothetical interactions:

"Little Johnny came home from school and found his dad in front of the television drinking beer. He told Dad that his teacher, Mrs. Pinkham, would flunk him if he didn't do his homework. Johnny's dad said, 'Mrs. Pinkham, that old bag. She flunked me too.'

"Contrast that to this. Johnny came home. His dad heard him and closed his study book. Johnny said Mrs. Pinkham was going to flunk him if he didn't do his homework. Johnny's dad covered his book with his hand. Then he thought about it and said, 'Johnny, I didn't do my homework when I was in school and I can't help you with your home-work.' Johnny's dad removed his hand to reveal his literacy workbook and said, 'Mom will be home soon, and we'll get her to help both of us.'

"Does that help? We've got to break the cycle of ignorance and it's got to start with the children. And we can only approach the children if we can convince the parents that there is a better way. Psychologists will confirm that the first eight or nine years of a child's life are extremely influential in forming the rest of their lives," Roberta said.

"That's pretty scary when you consider how unprepared too many parents are," Sandy said.

"That pretty much sums it up. I doubt if any parent is innocent when it comes to denying options to their children," Paul said.

"It's true, early childhood lessons are difficult to overcome, and we should use that knowledge to maintain social norms," Jerry said.

"All social norms?" Ashley asked.

"What do you mean?" Roberta asked.

"Christmas and Easter are inculcated into our social norms. And those social activities extend well beyond the Christian communities."

"Is that bad?" Roberta asked.

"Given my father's radical religion, I consider those institutions part of the big lie," Ashley said.

"Christmas is wonderful. How could we deny our daughter Christmas?" Roberta asked.

"There lies the problem. You celebrate it, your parents celebrated it, and your grandparents celebrated it, and you're determined to have your daughter celebrate it," Ashley said.

"Tell me. How is Christmas part of the big lie?" Rick asked, obviously looking for some enlightenment.

"Well, it seems to me, you have to start with the basics. What is Christmas? It's the celebration by Christians of an immaculate conception. Stop right there and think about it. *Immaculate conception?* That's against the very basis of all life on earth. It's impossible." Then Ashley hesitated and looked around the circle before she continued. "I consider it the biggest lie ever told. I know, I know. It's considered a miracle. Yet, how many millions are willing to die to defend a miracle. By definition a miracle opposes scientific laws and can only be explained by divine intervention. That's a circular argument; a logical fallacy. I can't base my life on a logical fallacy. If we believe in miracles we should just sit here and wait for divine intervention to deliver us. And while you're at it, consider the *resurrection*. A second-place big lie," Ashley said.

"Wow, Ashley. That's pretty strong, but at the same time, something many Christians have never reconciled. There must be a way to differentiate between a lie and belief in a miracle," Sandy said.

Rick then meekly asked, "But what if I choose to believe?"

"You can believe anything you want. Why should anyone care what you believe? The fact that you believe won't affect our relationship at all. What causes me great consternation is when believers promulgate arguments, rules, laws, and legislation based on their beliefs rather than on scientific knowledge. When that happens, my personal and civil rights are violated. It violates a basic tenet of the constitution—'the separation of church and state,'" Ashley answered.

"I find it offensive when someone tries to recruit me to their miracle beliefs," Sandy said.

"But, whether you settle on a lie or a miracle, how do you relate that to options for our children?" Jerry asked.

"From age one you bombard your daughter with Christmas lights, happy music, yule logs, Santa Claus, and presents. Then about age four, five, six, somewhere in there you admit that Santa Claus didn't really come down the chimney. Unbelievably, you refuse to admit the rest of the story is a myth as well. Then, along comes Easter and the kids all have a good time chasing eggs on the lawn and getting their chocolate. How do you expect them not to believe the big lie?" Ashley asked.

"That's pretty harsh, Ashley," Roberta said.

Ashley knew her comment was harsh and a bit too far for almost any group. She also admitted that she, too, enjoyed the spirit of the holidays, good tidings, and joy to all, but that it was based on a great hoax. "Do you deny it?" she asked.

Roberta involuntarily moved her arm forward, halted the movement, and then rested her elbow back on her knee. She opened her mouth but didn't speak. She held a perplexed look on her face for several seconds. Everybody waited for her response. "No, no I guess I don't."

"Isn't it possible to celebrate the holidays without believing in the immaculate conception?" Jerry asked.

"It seems to me, when we celebrate Christmas, we're perpetuating an irreconcilable event. But I'll admit we market it effectively," Sandy said.

"The holidays? How about a realistic holiday? There are several to choose from. I always liked a solstice party. A celebration based on ancient history and how our ancestors calculated the winter solstice. Many cultures computed it independently," Ben said.

"Ohhhh. I'm going to have to struggle with this," Roberta said. "I'm afraid I can't admit that I've been deceiving myself all these years. Maybe I've been guilty of ignoring the simple facts right before my very eyes. Social norms seem to be an excuse for taking the easy way out. I'm going to struggle with this. I've ignored this dilemma all my life. No, I don't believe in the immaculate conception, never have. But I failed to follow that to a resolution. If you won't accept a lie, or a miracle, or whatever; what do you do? What's the difference between telling a lie and supporting a lie?" Roberta asked.

"Maybe there's a difference between supporting a myth and ignoring a myth," Paul said.

"Not in any of my writings. I've always argued that if you ignore a lie, you're supporting it. Just like racism. If you don't fight it, you're supporting it—therefore a racist."

"Okay, I'll go along with that," Paul said.

"I've got some big apologies to make. Many of my readers are going to struggle with what I will have to write," Roberta said.

"How can you have any respect for a liar?" Rick asked.

"You can't. And nobody else should. And think about why you could possibly have any respect for anybody that makes excuses for a liar or a hypocrite," Roberta said.

"Hypocrisy is as dishonest as a lie," Sandy said.

"It reflects a weakness of character. If you believed it last week you better believe it this week or bring some new facts that justify a change in position," Jerry said.

"Like I said, I've got a lot of apologies to make. Some readers will even rejoice in seeing me struggle," Roberta repeated.

Eric and Connor left the fire and walked to their tent. They found their way into their sleeping bags and Eric whispered, "You know, these guys are no dummies. They know what makes the world work."

"I wanted to ask them if there were ever times a politician could justify telling less than the truth. It seems to me there are times when you can't just tell everybody everything you know."

"I think you're right. Bring it up some time," Eric said.

"Remember what Dad told us about how the military dealt with it? 'I could answer that, but then I would have to kill you.'"

"Yeah, and how to deal with rumors or misinformation—'consider the source and laugh it off.'"

The embers faded to bright ashes as the tense discussion shifted to their continuing condition of an uncertain trip. Jerry said, "I guess there's no telling what we'll get into tomorrow."

"You never know. The river changes all the time. The water probably won't get any deeper," Tom said. That was as positive as Tom could make it. The other way to say it would be that the water will be shallower, and they would have to portage around it. That was enough for the night. Everybody retired.

CHAPTER 13

*P*aul and Sandy started the day by themselves, rekindling the fire and preparing a sparse breakfast. A light breeze blew through a high overcast. Tom joined them briefly before he walked down the riverbank a hundred yards and climbed a low hillock to inspect the river. He wasn't sure, but it appeared that they'd be able to paddle for at least the first part of the morning.

Breakfast, boat launch, load, and paddle. The boat carried them ever closer to help. The overcast thickened and the sky blended with the horizon. Even the river and the landscape views merged with the sky. Tom steered into the main channel and the crew paddled efficiently. Practice made nearly perfect. Two hours down the river, confused channels forced Tom to maneuver near the riverbank to keep the boat in flowing deep water. The good paddling ended when the river widened out again.

The depth allowed safe passage until Ashley alerted Tom that there appeared to be something in the main channel. Tom stared down the river through the murky air and recognized the problem: a tree with snags, submerged in the channel. Tom ordered the paddlers to stop the boat and back up. They tried. The current seemed to strengthen and resisted their efforts. Tom encouraged them against the current; this was a serious threat. The boat slowed, but the channel overpowered their efforts and the boat moved toward the hazard. Tom yelled to them to use their paddles to push off the snags. They tried to move the boat around the snags, and Tom asked them to use their paddles to push off the tree again. This time Tom's voice was intentionally calm. If the worst event came to pass, he couldn't afford for anyone to panic. The crew knew what they had to do. Tom's presence gave the crew the courage to make every effort. Nobody panicked. They almost made it work.

One underwater snag caught the boat skin and ripped a two-foot gash in the tent fabric. The boat began to take on water. Even with water entering their rescue vessel, nobody panicked. That in itself was success. Tom told Eric to stuff and hold a waterproof coat on the ripped fabric. Then he told the paddlers to paddle hard toward the riverbank. When they reached the gravel bank, Ashley and Walt jumped out and held the boat away from more possible danger while all except Tom and Eric went ashore. Tom handed all packs, boat parts, and boxes to the crew on shore. With that done, Tom jumped out and motioned for Eric to do the same. The crew worked together, lifting and carrying the boat onto the shore and inverting it to inspect it and make repairs if possible.

Without prompting, Eric asked Tom how much time they had available to hunt before the boat would be ready. Tom guessed at least two hours and told them food would be more important than a quick exit. Eric and Connor took the rifle and developed a hunt plan. Low, undulating landscape growing small brushy plants plus decreased visibility didn't encourage the hunters. But they knew they couldn't bypass any opportunity to find some food. It was their responsibility.

Paul and Sandy nervously searched through the supply boxes. Finally, they found the tent repair kits along with saved pieces of tent material. They also found a sewing kit. The ragged hole in the bottom of their boat disappointed everyone and, at best, delayed their trip through the wilderness. They understood that the boat was their most likely means of escape. The success so far had caused everybody to put their faith in that boat.

Tom went to work. First, he assured the integrity of the wooden ribs, then he dried the area around the gash and inspected the repair materials. Orderly work ensued. With no broken or displaced ribs, this would be a minor interruption. Tom threaded a needle and stitched across the rough edges of the damaged tent material. Then he stitched and glued new material over the damaged area. Paul and Sandy stood by and sighed in relief when he told them they could make it good as new. The only damage was time lost. Not that a delay didn't extend their vulnerability. It did, but at this point, two or three hours didn't seem fatal. A good supply of repair-kit materials allowed Tom to work with confidence. With repairs in place, Tom advised everybody to rest while the glue dried.

"So, Sandy, what was your life before the restaurant?" Jerry asked.

"Before I met Paul, I guess I learned to depend on myself. And like Ashley, I had support at school. Not just teachers, but other students."

"That doesn't sound like a lot of self-dependency," Jerry said.

"Friends and teacher support started and ended at school. And at a few friends' houses."

"Popular and with friends. That sounds like a pretty good start," Rick said.

"Think about that, Rick. That's all there was."

"Do you want to talk about your home life?" Walt asked.

"I never want to talk about it. There wasn't much home life. I could never have my friends come home after school."

"No?" Rick didn't understand anything other than a normal childhood. Ashley's depiction of her homelife shocked him a little, but he assumed that was a one-off. His parents always welcomed his friends. That's the way it was supposed to be.

"I could never risk bringing a friend home to my mother who might be drunk. I cooked most of the family dinners during my high school years. I couldn't wait to get out of there."

"How did you make it out?" Jerry asked.

"After graduation, I got a job waiting tables, moved out, and put myself through state college."

"Wow, nothing is ever easy, is it?" Ashley asked.

"How did you meet Paul?" Roberta asked.

"After I graduated, I went to work for a concert promoter. It was good work for a few years. As usual practice, I went to post concert parties. You can imagine the good times and personalities. One night after a particularly good show, I met Paul, who managed the rock band that highlighted the night. We had chemistry almost from first sight. I wanted some adventure and Paul wanted to quit cross-country trips with no real home. In the morning, he left with the band and we started a long-distance relationship. We lived vicariously in each other's world for a couple of years. Paul moved a few things into my apartment and flew in when the band was close. I flew to a few interesting concerts. It served us well for a while."

"That's not training for a real restaurant," Jerry said.

"No. We decided we wanted to find something we could do together. That was the most important thing for us. We knew we wanted to get married and decided to save our money, learn, and explore the opportunities. We agreed on a restaurant and I started culinary school in my free time."

"Good planning, good work, good success," Paul proudly said.

"Did you ever get your adventure?" Roberta asked.

"I think this is it."

"This would fill the bill," Walt said.

Tom acknowledged Eric and Connor when they returned to the boat and merely shook their heads. Nobody displayed disappointment. They launched the boat and started again. Neither Eric nor Connor repeated anything they talked about while hunting, but they were impressed with how calmly Tom reacted to the emergency boat repair. He just went to work with the task at hand. Their serious discussion also gave them an incentive to get closer to their fellow passengers.

The weather remained dull and overcast. Tom decided to make up some lost time by paddling until almost dark. He knew his crew would be able to set up a quick camp without much light. The sky was almost clear, and the partial moon was bright. The crew had demonstrated strength and an uncanny ability to work together that impressed Tom.

He directed efforts to bring the boat onto the riverbank. A series of rocks made the landing difficult and a little dangerous for the boat. With everybody out of the boat safely, they lifted it out and away from the rocks. A good supply of firewood littered the ground near the campsite and after dinner they situated themselves around a comfortable fire. Eric and Connor didn't join them.

Rick stood across the fire from Roberta. "Roberta, what did you study in college?"

"I was a math major, why?"

"I was wondering about how you got to your ideas on politics and logic things."

"Do you want to get into politics?"

"Not necessarily. When I go back to school in the spring, I might want to take some classes that would emphasize logical thinking. I'm impressed with how all of you have strong opinions that you can defend."

"Logical thinking's important, regardless of any major you choose," Ben said.

"You can go straight to logic classes, philosophy, or mathematics. There is nothing more logical than mathematics. Try not to get yourself stuck in the kind of quandary I've fallen into, regarding Christmas, social norms, and hypocrisy," Roberta said cryptically. She had obviously been struggling with her problem.

"Where're Eric and Connor? I wonder what they studied," Rick asked.

"Why don't you go ask them to join us out here?" Sandy asked.

Rick wasn't sure if Sandy was sincere, but he went to their tent to ask them to join the group at the fire. "They're not in their tent," Rick called back to the crew at the fire. "Oh, they're working down by the river."

"I wonder what they're doing. I'll go down there," Tom said. Tom and Rick went to the river and found Eric and Connor had moved enough rocks so that launching the boat in the morning would be safer for the boat and easier for the crew to board. Rick and Tom helped finish the job and returned to the fire with them.

"I wish I'd been paying more attention. All of us should have been down there helping you. Good job," Tom said to Eric and Connor, loud enough for the rest of the camp to hear.

"What happened?" Jerry asked.

"They reworked the landing spot. Tomorrow's launch will be a piece of cake," Rick answered.

"Well, we should have been helping. Thank you, guys," Paul said.

Eric and Connor found spots in front of the fire. "We like clean landings. Our boat's not fragile like this one, but we're always careful not to bang it up," Eric said.

"So, you're sailors too?" Sandy asked.

"We have a world-class sailboat in the lake."

"What brand?" Roberta asked.

"A fifty-foot Swan?"

"Wow. That's a lot of boat for a lake," Roberta said. "We've got a forty-five-foot Norseman in Seattle."

"That's a nice boat," Connor said.

"So is the Swan. Do you race or cruise?" Jerry asked.

"We have a pretty good reputation in our club when it comes to racing. What do you do with your boat?" Connor asked.

"We spend a lot of weekends cruising in the San Juans. We've taken it up the inside passage to Alaska, and once we circumnavigated Vancouver Island," Roberta answered.

"Who does the navigation?" Eric asked.

"Jerry does the navigation. I just steer a straight course. How does your team work?"

"We trade off."

"What kinds of races do you win?" Roberta asked.

"Half-day to three-day events," Connor answered.

"Have you ever taken her out to the North Atlantic?" Paul asked.

"No."

"Why not? You've got a boat that could go anywhere," Jerry asked.

"That would take a big commitment."

In her relentless style, Roberta asked, "What's the problem with a commitment?"

"Nothing, for most people. We just pick and choose what we want to do," Eric said.

"Have you ever done anything you didn't want to do?" Sandy asked.

"Not since we got out of school," Connor answered, quite frankly.

"I guess that doesn't count fighting for our lives out here," Eric said.

"Yeah, that's a little different for all of us," Paul said.

"What school did you attend?" Sandy asked.

"We both graduated from the University of Illinois," Connor said.

"What did you name your boat?" Sandy asked.

"*Ercon.*"

"Makes sense."

"You know the old saying, 'A ship is safe at harbor, but that is not what ships are for'? I always liked that saying. Whenever I wonder if I should take a chance, I recite that, and then decide," Roberta said.

"Yeah, it got you out here," Connor said.

"That's the point. I could be at home baking cookies and watching television from my easy chair. And then I would miss all this. Landscape, wildlife, new friends, adventure—life on the edge," Roberta said.

"And, maybe death," Connor said.

"Okay, and maybe not. And when we get back, think of the memories we'll all have."

"It's true, we all have reasons to get back. People we miss, people that will miss us. The real question is are you afraid to die?" Ashley asked.

"Why is that the question?" Eric asked.

"You know, I've lived out here most of my life. The people I know here, including my parents, would never be afraid to die. My dad talked to me about that. He told me if I was afraid to die, I'd never amount to anything. He said if I lived well, there was nothing to fear. It makes me feel a little better, knowing my parents weren't afraid to die," Tom said.

"I think your father had it right. If you're afraid of your own shadow, you miss out on life," Roberta said.

Sandy stared into the fire and focused on a single ember. As she studied the intensity of the white-hot cinder, she analyzed its life cycle. Soon it would die. Ashes would be its legacy. She thought about life—going along safely or burning brightly, even if only a short time. Then she refocused on the ember and its alternative destiny, a wet, cold, and moldering piece of driftwood on the riverbank. She agreed, living brightly if only a short time was the better alternative. "Living well and brightly is the key. A dull life has no value. You might as well be dead." Sandy then recited her thoughts about the ember and its alternatives.

"So, you think we should take our boat out into the open ocean?" Connor asked.

"That's up to you. You've got a boat that would handle it and you seem to be good sailors," Jerry said.

"Let's concentrate on the boat we've got now," Eric said.

"That's a good idea. Even if there's a possibility of dying, we don't have to accept it lying down," Paul said.

"Ashley, you sounded like you needed to get back alive earlier. Now, you sound like you're not afraid to die. How do you reconcile that?" Rick asked.

"We've all got a reason and desire to get home. But, if I don't make it—well, like Sandy said, better to live brightly for a short time than to live a dull life. Remember what Paul said, we're not giving up easily. If

I die, I want to go out like that ember, not moldering and whimpering away on the soggy riverbank."

"If we just keep working together, I think we'll be okay. Let's get ready for tomorrow," Tom said.

CHAPTER 14

The day began the way the evening had ended, in good spirits. They launched the boat at the improved landing area and loaded it with ease. All aboard, they paddled toward safety and home. Three hours of steady paddling brought them to shallow riffles, too shallow for safe passage. Low clouds grew darker. The river broadened out and lacked a navigable channel. Several small gravel islands grew out of the shallow water. Tom thought a channel they could navigate emerged about a hundred yards down the river.

They discussed two options. They could carry packs, supplies, and equipment fifty yards to the solid riverbank by wading through the shallow water, then carry everything down the riverbank, and then wade back through the shallow water to the boat after floating the empty boat through the riffles. Or, they could unload everything onto an island in the middle of the river, float the empty boat over the riffles, then carry everything through the riffles to the waiting boat. They decided to carry everything down through the riffles.

Once everything rested on a small island in the middle of the broad river, it began to rain. Tom and Ben secured the boat with ropes and guided it down the riffles. As expected, the river regrouped and provided a channel acceptable to paddle at the end of the hundred-yard stretch of riffles. Tom waved to the rest of the crew, giving them the okay to bring supplies and equipment by wading down the riffles. That trek was no fun, although not as bad as the portage over the hill. The current strength wasn't enough to sweep the wading trekkers off their feet, but it was enough to keep them on guard. Obtuse irregular sized stones made the footholds insecure. Of course, wading against the current provided a physical challenge. Back and forth and two hours later, they were ready to resume paddling through the light wind and rain.

Two more hours and the boat approached the entrance to the Porcupine River. The Porcupine was an important landmark for Tom. He knew they could make it out. If they cut back on the remaining food, they could make it without going into starvation mode. After all, anybody could stand a little hunger. Tom decided to cross the river and camp on the opposite bank even though they still had over an hour of good light. The wind and increasing rain made it difficult to navigate on the big river.

The crew followed the usual procedures for hauling out. They carefully lifted the boat onto an expansive gravel bar. Then they carried the boat away from the river to higher ground, inverted it, and set up their tents nearby. Those tasks had become routine and required minimal effort. Tom talked about the remainder of the trip. There would be no more portages. Two more days of paddling and they would be close to the Yukon where he said they would find human activity. Work in the wind and rain didn't allow the campers to celebrate or even fully appreciate the good news. Paul and Sandy prepared a cup of soup for everyone and served a small amount of smoked fish with it. They found enough firewood to build a healthy fire under the tarp and tried to keep warm as darkness set in. The wind and rain intensified, and the campers gave up trying to fight it and went to bed. As usual, Ashley and Tom used the boat as their refuge while everybody else shared a tent. The rain continued, and the wind intensified.

After hours of unsettled sleep with gusting wind and rain, the campers' fate turned horribly bad. A ferocious gust of wind lifted the inverted boat like an airfoil then forced it back down violently in the worst possible position. The gunwale landed on Tom's head and chest. The aft section landed on Ashley's midsection. Another gust lifted the boat again and smashed it down on the rocks, breaking the gunwale and several ribs. Then the wind swept the boat along the gravel before a broken gunwale stick tangled in Jerry and Roberta's tent ropes. Jerry climbed out onto the beach. Roberta didn't make it out. She screamed as the boat, now resembling more a kite than a boat, dragged her and the tent toward the water. The shape of the boat began to disintegrate, but the skin, caught in the wind, pulled Roberta, in her tent, into the water. Eric and Connor heard the screams and jumped out of their tent. Jerry yelled, "She's in the tent!"

Eric and Connor ran to the river and jumped in. Walt followed them into the river, chasing Roberta and the tent. Eric tried to get control of the flailing boat skin while Connor found the tent and searched in the dark for a zippered flap to get Roberta out. Walt grabbed a line from the boat and tried to help Eric control the boat's remnants. Connor found the opening flap and spread it, hoping Roberta could reach out to him. He shouted into the tent. Roberta yelled, "Help!" Connor pushed his head and shoulders into the tent, which was filling with water, and reached out in the dark water to find her. He felt an arm and pulled her to the exit. He got her out of the tent and told Eric he had her. Eric said he couldn't hold the boat. Walt's boat line pulled him underwater in his attempts to hold the boat for Connor. He didn't hear Connor acknowledge that he got Roberta out. Connor screamed to let the boat go and help get Roberta to the gravel bank. When Eric released the boat part he was holding, it collapsed into the river and tangled Walt underneath in the water.

Jerry met them at the water's edge. He helped Connor carry Roberta back to the mostly destroyed camp. Paul and Sandy crawled out of their tent and realized that without weight, it would blow away. They began moving food and supplies into the tent. Ben went to his tent and told

Rick to secure it. Within minutes, the heavy gusts quit, and it stopped raining. Rick joined the group surrounding Roberta.

Roberta stood on the bank, shivering.

"Are you okay?" Eric asked.

Roberta put her hands to her head and then nodded her head. "I think so."

"We need to get her dry and warm. Jerry, take her to our tent, get her clothes off, and get her into a sleeping bag," Ben said.

"Where's Tom and Ashley?" Connor asked.

"Where's Walt?" Ben shouted.

"Tom and Ashley were sleeping under the boat," Paul said.

"Walt was in the river with us. We must find him. Come on, Eric!" Connor shouted. Ben ran to the river with the brothers and shouted for Walt. No answer.

"I'm going down the riverbank until I find him," Ben shouted.

"We're coming with you," Eric said. They made their way along the dark, rough, and slippery riverbank. Their shouts went unanswered. Ben fought the dark, rocks, and brush close to the water. His bare feet suffered cuts and scrapes as he continued to call for Walt. Eric and Connor were just as determined.

"We can't see much out here. Keep talking so we know we're all here," Connor said.

"Ben, how far away are you?" Eric shouted.

"Over here, in the water. I can't see much." Ben's voice came back from only about ten yards away.

"Stay where you are. Let's stay together as we make our way down the river," Connor said. The Porcupine River was a lot more water than the small river they had been paddling in. The deep water and swift current disheartened them. Eric and Connor fought through the brush to Ben with one foot in the water.

"It'll be safer if we move down this together," Eric said. They continued to inch their way down the river, available to each other with a helping hand when needed. After two hours of painstaking travel down the river, the sky began to lighten enough to allow them to analyze the river.

"Look, down there," Ben said. A hundred and fifty yards down the river they identified the boat skin. They wrestled their way to it. Ben waded into the water and pulled the mass of tangled nylon away from a tree branch partially submerged next to the gravel bank. Eric and Connor worked together to free the boat skin along with Jerry and Roberta's tent.

"Walt didn't get tangled in the boat. What could have happened to him?" Ben asked.

"Don't know. Shall we keep going?" Eric asked.

"I don't think it'll do any good. Look at that river. From here, for as far as I can see, it's straight and fast. Let's untangle this mess and get it back to camp. We'll hope he found his way back," Ben said.

While Ben, Eric, and Connor made their way down the river, the rest of the crew had gone to where the boat had been and saw Tom, not moving, wrapped in his waterproof tarp. Ashley attempted to sit up, still in her sleeping bag, but pain didn't allow it. Paul and Sandy tended to Ashley while Jerry and Rick went to Tom.

"How is she?" Paul asked.

"It seems like the boat landed on her ribs. She's probably got a broken rib or two," Sandy said.

"Is she spitting up any blood?" Paul asked.

Ashley closed her mouth and tasted her saliva. "I can't taste any blood," she said.

"Let's clear out the tent and put her in there," Paul said.

"Tom, talk to me," Jerry said.

Only Tom's head protruded from the tarp. Jerry reached out and touched his head. When he retrieved his hand, it was smeared with blood. "He's bleeding from his head again. Let's carry him over and put him in the tent with Roberta."

Jerry convinced himself that Roberta was safe before helping get Tom into the tent.

"What's the situation, Paul?" Jerry asked.

"We've got Ashley in our tent. She's probably got a couple of broken ribs. Tom's got blood on his head and isn't responding. Walt is missing. We have to try to find him."

Jerry said, "Okay, I want constant care for Tom and Ashley. I think Roberta's going to be okay. Sandy, take some water and stay with Ashley. Give her a little water when she wants it. Paul, get some water and watch Tom. Talk to him often and let me know if he responds. How much food did we lose?"

"We got what we had stacked outside back into our tent to keep the tent from blowing away. Now, I've got most of it outside again."

"That's a piece of good news. Does anybody else have any injuries?" Nobody answered. "I'll take that as another piece of good news. Okay, there's not much we can do until the sun comes up."

Jerry huddled up next to a small willow bush near the tent with Tom and Rick. He tried to contemplate what the morning would bring. There would be concern and then some decisions to make. His thoughts for Tom brought a constant reminder. Indecision would kill them. He would consider the circumstances, measure the options, listen to suggestions, and make decisions. He listened to Rick ask Tom questions for nearly an hour before the sky began to lighten. Tom never answered. Jerry hoped he would at least be able to ask Tom some questions before he had to make decisions.

Daylight broke and Jerry felt a slight sense of relief as he scanned the horizon and stared into the rising sun. Minimal overcast and little more than a light breeze blew through the camp. Three tents stood in place and plenty of firewood littered the area. After concern for the whereabouts of Walt and the condition of Tom and Ashley, the missing boat, Ben, Eric, and Connor caused immediate anxiety. The long limbs they would need to build another boat weren't available here on this riverbank, only a multitude of small irregular sticks. Vegetation consisted mostly of low-growing willows and other small bushes. Jerry assumed Ben, Walt, Eric, and Connor were miserable, cold, and wet, but alive. He at least hoped Walt was with them.

Jerry gathered some wood they had protected from the rain and started a fire.

A half hour later, Rick opened the flap to the tent and called for Jerry. "Tom's coming around."

Jerry went to the tent and called in. "Tom, can you understand me?"

"Uh-huh?"

"A storm came up last night and destroyed the boat. Part of it hit you on the head and you've been unconscious."

"Oh, mmm?"

"The boat and Jerry's tent are gone. Ashley got hurt too when the boat blew away."

Tom tried to speak but couldn't find the strength.

"Stay where you are. I'll bring you something soon."

Jerry crawled out of the tent and scanned the river, downstream. Unbeknownst to him, Ben, Eric, and Connor were continuing their struggle to bring the boat remnants back.

"Paul, can you cook up some soup? Then we have to make some decisions," Jerry said.

Jerry took two small cups of soup to Ashley and Roberta, then talked to Paul about a short-term plan before returning to check on Ashley and Roberta.

Fortunately, Roberta had gone to bed fully dressed. The only problem was that now she was in the sleeping bag and her clothes, which had been removed, were soaking wet. Jerry asked Paul to wring them out and hang them near the fire where they wouldn't burn. Ashley was dressed and sitting up, sipping her soup. Jerry asked how her ribs felt. She said it only hurt when she laughed. Jerry asked Sandy if she thought it would help if they wrapped Ashley's ribs. Sandy said she thought it might be a good idea, so he asked her to see if she could find the materials and do that.

Jerry returned to the fire with Paul and made decisions about the campsite, hoping Tom could join them soon. Jerry would know more about hiking conditions when Ben, Eric, and Connor returned, but he didn't know whether it was feasible for everybody to try to walk out. Ashley and Tom were serious considerations. Maybe he should designate two people to hike out for help. He wished Tom could help him with his knowledge of the area. They decided to start another fire just out of the camp as a signal fire. That fire would be kept burning day and night. They also cut fresh green vegetation that would smoke when thrown on the fire. They would do that when they saw or heard an airplane.

Sandy came to Jerry and reported that Tom was trying to talk in the tent. Jerry thought that was good news. He went to Tom and asked how he was doing. Tom stumbled on his words. His voice was weak and barely audible. Jerry told Tom about Ashley, where the crew was working, what he'd done, and about the signal fire. Then Jerry asked Tom about the possibilities of walking out. In the weakest voice, Tom gave him the bad news. Most of area between them and Fort Yukon was either swampy or vulnerable to flooding in a heavy rain. Following the river would be rough and dangerous all the way. It appeared that waiting and hoping for an airplane would be their only real option. The last few words were almost unintelligible; it sounded like "irch lanier . . . gather." Tom closed his eyes. Jerry realized Tom's situation was more serious than he'd imagined.

Jerry put his hand on Tom's head briefly, then crawled out of the tent.

An hour later, Jerry was relieved to see Ben, Eric, and Connor returning with a heavy load. He trotted down the riverbank to help them. He asked about Walt.

"There was no sign of him. How am I going to explain this to Joan?" Ben cried.

"I'm sorry, Ben. We're all sorry. I don't know what to say," Jerry said.

"How's Ashley and Tom?" Ben asked after wiping the tears away.

"Ashley's probably got a couple broken ribs and Tom's in serious condition," Jerry answered. The four men trudged despondently back to camp.

Roberta heard Eric and Connor and asked to see them. They went into Roberta's tent. She sat up and wrapped her arms around them. "Thank you. I haven't even thanked you yet. You saved my life. You risked your lives to save me. I will never forget that. Thank you."

"We're in this together now. We were worried about getting you out of there. It was tricky."

"It was dangerous. You were brave, beyond compare," Roberta replied.

"We're in this together. We lost Walt. I'm having a hard time with that," Eric said. Roberta closed her eyes and wiped away what would have been a tear. Sandy, still in the tent caring for Roberta, closed her eyes and shook her head softly. She would have cried, but she had joined the stoic atmosphere in the camp.

Eric and Connor had rolled all the recovered nylon and other material together for easier transport back to camp, so now the campers unrolled most of the skin from the boat and Jerry's tent, complete with his sleeping bag and clothes for him and Roberta. All they had to do was to let it all dry. They quickly stretched the tattered boat-skin remnants over their lean-to, which would give them much better protection from wind and rain.

Eric and Connor recovered their clothes and retrieved their gun from the gravel outside their tent. They said they were going hunting. "We'll be back before dark."

As agreed, Eric and Connor returned to camp before dark, but they returned disappointed. Eric said they found nothing and that they would try again in the morning and hunt down the river.

Wet clothes and sleeping bags hung around the fire and would dry in time—in some cases, a lot of time. Time was better than getting wet items too close to the fire. They couldn't afford to waste anything. Jerry made every decision in line with that thought. He talked to Paul and Sandy and asked them to inventory the food and create diets that would maximize nutrition and energy for three days. Without new food sources, three days was the maximum. When actual needs didn't present themselves, Jerry found tasks around camp to keep his charges busy enough to avoid dwelling on their predicament. One of his fears was that as starvation set in, bad decisions could override plans that had otherwise been approved. Hunger could instigate desperation.

CHAPTER 15

The first full day after they lost the boat, Eric and Connor concentrated their hunt downriver. Rick and Ben would scout another section, up the riverbank, for game. They carried the pistol and hoped they could use it effectively if there was game out. The hunters left camp at first light.

Eric and Connor stalked through the brush twenty yards apart. They thought that would give them a better chance of finding any tracks they could follow. Staying within a close distance was safer yet gave them coverage. After three hours of searching with no positive results, they climbed a small hillock that gave them visual command of the area. The view from the hillock gave them a much greater area to search than the restricted views from within the bushes. They sat back to back and concentrated on identifying any sign of movement around them. It was a good plan.

"We can't afford to miss anything," Eric said.

"When we see some movement, we'll find a way to get to it." Quiet time on the hillock gave them an opportunity to think and contemplate their existence. "It makes me sick to think of Walt. How could we have saved him?"

"I wish I could have done something. I didn't see what happened. We were all vulnerable there in the water. He must have gotten tangled in the boat skin, trying to find Roberta. I'm like you. It makes me sick.

I'm missing him." The words—and more importantly, the thoughts—flowed freely. Eric didn't try to mince or hide his feelings.

"I hope Tom snaps out of it. He doesn't look good. We need to keep him as stable as we can until we can get him medical. Not only for him but for all of us. Jerry's doing everything he can for him. The one person that means the most to survival is in serious condition," Connor said.

"I think Jerry's doing everything he can for all of us. Remember how Tom got after him because he didn't take charge after the earthquake? I'm not sure what that was about, but he's taking charge now. I'm impressed. It takes a lot of pressure off the rest of us. We can do what we can without worrying about what's going on back at camp. He makes it a team effort. His wife's a force too. Yeah, at first, I thought she was a pain, but she knows what she's talking about. One thing that's rather impressive is her willingness to question herself. She thinks. And she makes everybody else think too. If thinking is in force, she can deal with it. You don't have to agree with her. Just formulate a concise thought and work it out. I've been noodling on that. I'd like to write about some of our discussions. If we make it out of here, I'm thinking maybe I'll write my first novel."

"You going to write about this trip?"

"I'm thinking about centering it on Roberta and the way she approaches options and decision-making. And in the end, a person honest enough to question her own foundation. I think there's a lot of potential there."

"If you're going to do that, I might try to develop some melodies I've been playing with on the river into a symphonic score. I'd like to grow into something closer to Jerry and Roberta than where I see us heading. They're reasonable, personable, and they've made commitments. I'd like to spend some time with them after we make it out," Connor said.

"They're an interesting couple. There's some depth there. Paul and Sandy are of the same mold in a lot of ways. They've played in the real world, struggled, and made it to the top. They're also good team players.

I feel good about them taking care of the food. They know what they're doing." Then Eric took a deep breath and exhaled slowly. On his next breath, he told Connor he respected the commitment Paul and Sandy had made to the restaurant business. They had considered the options and decided on their business future, along with making a long-term commitment to their relationship.

"I'd like to build something," Eric continued. "Probably not a restaurant. Maybe a novel would fill that void. I'm going to do it."

"Sandy has been a force in directing her own life. Imagine her homelife during high school. She was strong and focused on what she wanted. She made it happen. This adventure is good for us. We're seeing real people, people we can depend on. And they trust us to do our best too. It feels good, being on a team. How did we miss out on this for so long?" Connor wondered aloud.

"We let money we didn't earn set the agenda. I'm not saying money is bad, but we can't let it control us."

"Do you want to start a business?"

"I don't know. For now, I'm going to write. After that, I don't know. I know my priorities have shifted substantially."

"Would you consider changing our boat's name?"

"Why?"

"I just thought we could start planning a new lifestyle."

"How would renaming the boat promote a change?"

"Maybe a daily reminder to see the world in a more realistic way."

"What would you change it to?"

"How about *Commitment*?"

Eric thought about that for a couple of breaths. "I think that's a good idea. Let's do it. Maybe a commitment to the open ocean too."

The brothers went silent for several minutes, all the while scanning the landscape. There were no signs of life in three hundred sixty degrees for as far as they could see.

"I'm comparing our tender years with what Sandy and Ashley lived through," Eric said.

"I wonder what Rick will do with his life," Connor said.

"He grew up in a protective, safe environment. He's seen the real world out here. He came here to learn a few things. Its been good for him, even if he got more than he signed up for."

"I don't think he'd trade it, though. He's soaking up a lot of life he's never been exposed to. He'll have some direction when he gets back."

"We'll stay in contact. I'm curious where his education will take him. Maybe we can help him."

"Let's keep that to ourselves for now," Connor said.

"What do you think of Ashley?"

"She's gay."

"So what? If all gay people can keep up with her, we should adjust our prejudices."

"You know they can't."

"No, no. Few straight people could ever hold a candle to her. But then, why do gay people have to be better to be accepted? What if they run the gamut of human strengths and fragilities like the rest of the world? Why should we care? How does it affect us? Think about what Roberta told us about the amygdala. Why should we fear them just because they're not exactly like us? What's to fear?" Eric asked.

"Good for you. That's something I've struggled with. I think I can fix it. Besides, think about what gay people are forced to give up, just to be who they are. Think about what our supposed friends, people at the yacht club for instance, would think if we announced that we were gay. It would be like white people announcing that we're all giving up all our 'white privilege.' Think about that for a while."

"White privilege . . . " Eric stopped and choked down an irritating thought. "White privilege, that's something we've had a lot of. When I think about it, I'm sort of ashamed of it. I think I need to work on it.

How would that rectify it? You can't just wear a sign saying 'don't extend white privilege to me.'"

"If you tried to talk to somebody about it, you'd hear something like 'hard work got me to where I am today.' How would you respond to that?" Connor asked.

Eric digested Connor's question but fell into the realization that this conversation transcended anything they had ever shared before. He wished his parents were available to validate and perhaps guide the discussion. After a deep and silent breath, he answered, "Good point. Well . . . maybe the point is that hard work has different results for different people."

"What do you mean?"

"If a white kid impressed somebody with hard work, he might be given an opportunity at a job with responsibility. Whereas, if Jorge's hard work is recognized, he's likely to get little more than an invitation to come back tomorrow for more. Hard work is good; looking and sounding like the boss is even better," Eric said.

Connor closed his eyes while he digested the ugly truth, then thought more about it. "We obviously receive privileges because we're white. That alone isn't enough. Privilege should be bestowed on everybody. No. That would be true equality. That's not going to happen. But it can't be delivered based on color. Who should receive privileges? Let's see. When I was good and you were bad, I got a cookie. That worked. You work hard, do what's right, you get a privilege cookie. I can live with that."

"A privilege cookie. Really?" Now Eric laughed. He understood and agreed with everything Connor said. "I'd like to talk to Roberta about that sometime."

"What if Ashley wasn't gay?"

"I went to sleep the other night thinking about that."

"Yeah, I bet."

"No. Not what you think. At least at this point in my life, I don't think I could be with her. Not that there's anything wrong with her. In fact, I think she's about perfect. I don't like to admit it, but in my new life and being honest, I would be intimidated. She's educated, has a good job, and she's overcome some obstacles that would crush lesser people. On top of that, she's done more physical work than we've ever thought about. Yes, I would be intimidated. She's so far ahead of any woman I've ever dated, I wouldn't have anything to say," Eric said.

"She's so good, I bet if she were interested, she could put you at ease."

"Well, we don't have to contemplate those possibilities. I still think she's a super person."

"I'm glad she's with us. We're all better off with her calm manner and skills in the wild. She way more than pulls her weight. She sure doesn't have any use for the big Christian miracles."

"It must have been miserable, living in that house with her father."

"Don't think that's a one-off household."

"Yeah, it's scary. These are all things I can write about. I wonder if I can fit it all together."

"You have to put Ben into your story."

"For sure. He's a lot like Ashley: strong, calm, capable."

"And you can be sure he's overcome a lot of racial stuff. It's amazing. We never had to put up with any of the stuff he lived with in Alabama. It makes me feel small to consider what we haven't done compared to what he's accomplished. Not only accomplished, but how he knows he doesn't have to prove anything. They couldn't beat a good man down," Connor said.

"We started with two giant steps ahead of him: money and white privilege. I think we can take some pride in that we never practiced racism, though."

"No, not outwardly, but maybe by not fighting it, we're guilty of complicity. I wish Dad were still alive. I'd like to have known him better. He always gave us the impression of being tough, but I think there was a lot more that we missed. The one thing I know he left us was his view on racism, that it wasn't acceptable."

"Do you know where that came from?" Eric asked.

"Mom talked about it once. She said he learned a lot about race while he was in the Marines. She said something about life and death and depending on each other." Connor thought back to some conversations with his father. His father never talked about combat, but he did talk about the corps, "Semper Fi," and honor. From what Connor could ascertain, his father's experience in the Marines Corps was one of his proudest times. "Eric, if I die out here, I'll do it in a way that would have made Dad proud. I'll die with honor, helping somebody else survive."

"That would be worthy for both of us, I think," Eric said. Then he thought for a few more moments and continued in a soft, flowing voice. "You know, this is the first time I've ever done any self-recrimination; I don't understand it. I've never even thought about being less than perfect until we met this group. It's like looking in the mirror and being honest. In a way, it feels good, realizing that we can fit in."

"There's some fear-based emotion here but I think I feel the same way. I don't just want to be with this group. I want to be a part of it. That's new for me to say, too.

"I haven't seen anything move out there. Do you want to hunt over to that next little hill? Maybe there's something on the other side."

"We don't want to be out here after dark, but I think we need to try. Let's go."

They spent an hour working through thick brush and then up another small hill. They took positions from which they could scan the area. Nothing moved. It was disappointing. The only positive thing they found from that vantage point was a way they could walk around the thick brush when they started back. Connor thought if they kept moving, they could get back before dark. Trudging back to camp encouraged more talk about their future and how they might address the rest of the campers. The smoke in the air gave them a direction finder.

CHAPTER 16

When Ashley moved, she moved purposefully and slowly. She wasn't going to do any rough work. Tom's head had suffered another nasty crushing blow above his ear from the boat. His skull appeared to be swollen. He looked like he'd been beaten severely. He wasn't responding and couldn't take food or water. Jerry consulted with Sandy. Sandy said she would tease some water through his lips. All Jerry could think to do was to continue to have all available hands collect all the firewood they could find. He added that plenty of green material should be available for producing smoke. That work continued until Ben and Rick returned from their reconnaissance.

"Did you see the plane?" Ben asked as he walked briskly into camp.

"No," Jerry answered.

"Where did you see it?"

"On the horizon, over there." Ben aligned the landmarks that he had identified in the field to accurately describe the location. Then he pointed to a specific spot across the great expanse.

"How long ago did you see it?" Jerry asked.

"I figure it would have been about two hours ago. We started back right after we saw it."

"That would make it about three hours after daylight. That makes sense. Tom told me Fort Yukon was over there. I wish we could talk to him. I didn't understand the last thing he told me. See if you can make sense out of it."

"After the boat landed on his head?" Ben asked.

"Yeah, the last weak sounds he made were something like 'irch lanier . . . gather.'"

Ben repeated the phrase and tried to make sense out of it. "Gather birch? There are no birch trees here. We should ask Eric and Connor if they've seen any birch trees. What would he mean by lanier?"

"So, we should keep smoke in the air every morning," Paul said.

"Yeah. At least. In fact, any time the sky is clear we should keep a lot of smoke in the air," Jerry said.

"We've got mostly clear air now. Let's make some smoke puffs." Jerry led the way to the signal fire, and they fueled it with dry wood. Then they threw green wood, leaves, and grass on the hot flames. Dark-gray smoke spiraled high into the air. The fact that the concept of smoke signals appeared to operate as planned gave everybody a sense of hope. The campers worked around their problems in camp for the rest of the day. As the sun disappeared, they began to worry about Eric and Connor.

"I wish Eric and Connor were back. It's going to be tough out there in the dark," Roberta said.

"Let's get a good blaze going in the signal fire. Maybe a little extra light will help," Jerry said. They did that, but it was unnecessary.

Just after dark, Eric and Connor returned to camp empty-handed. "We saw the smoke, anything new?"

"Ben and Rick saw a plane when they were out," Paul said.

They sat around the fire that night and ate their next-to-last meal. Silence prevailed until Eric stood and walked slowly around the fire. "Connor and I have been talking and we've had some revelations on our little trip down the river. If you're willing, we'd like to share some of it with the group," Eric said.

"We're all here, one for all, all for one," Roberta said.

"That's kind of what we wanted to share. And that's a saying we never used in our past lives. And furthermore, you were right when you figured we bought whatever friendship we had."

"That's not something I want to be known for," Roberta replied.

"Don't worry, it was good for us. Somebody stood up and told the truth about us. Everybody else has always been afraid we'd pull their funding. And we've done some funding. You're all independent and have no reason to kiss our asses. You might find it hard to believe, but that's something new to us. We realize that we maintained a close circle of people that were dependent upon us for one reason or another. People that would have looked the other way if we got into trouble and would have run if we asked for help."

"What Eric's trying to say is that we consider you our only true friends, people that would put their lives on the line for us. Until you came down the river, we weren't even seriously concerned about how we'd get home. We assumed someone would bail us out. That's how far out of touch with reality we were," Connor said.

"I think this whole adventure has given us all some new perspectives," Paul said.

"When we listen to you, we think we better understand what our father tried to teach us. He was faithful to his opinions, usually about power and money, but always consistent. We didn't worry much about whether we thought he was right or wrong, we just went along so we didn't have to justify anything to him. We think it's about time we try to build a foundation for our lives: friends we can depend on, opinions we can defend, and work we can be proud of," Connor said.

"I'm not sure we can say we always live up to that, but we can probably say we try," Roberta said.

"Trying is better than running from it," Paul said.

"What did you study at the university?" Sandy asked.

"I have an English degree and Connor graduated with a degree in music theory."

"Have you ever done anything with that education?" Jerry asked.

"Not yet. I tried to compile famous or infamous quotations once but gave it up when someone told me it wasn't very original," Eric said.

"Still talking about commitments. We've decided to do something you made us realize we always wanted to do. We always wanted to sail around the world. We just couldn't get around to making a life-sized commitment. We're going to do it. And, in your honor, we're renaming our boat *Commitment*," Connor added.

"Well then, I guess we better get home," Roberta said.

"Not only that, but Connor is going to put some of his melodies together with his musical expertise and write his symphony number one. And, in my thinking and spare time on the boat, I'll write my first novel. A novel about psychological survival and options set in a physically challenging life-and-death situation."

"That's a commitment," Ben said.

"Sounds familiar," Paul said.

"We'll consider this helping you with the research," Jerry said.

"I'm glad I could be a part of it," Ashley said.

"Your book would have been a fun read. Wish we had it here now," Paul said.

"It's the original and totally unexpected twist that puts our minds in a dither. It's an example of how laughter is the best remedy. Rather than say 'How stupid,' we usually laugh about a totally preposterous proposition," Eric said.

"Well said, Eric," Jerry said.

"Sometimes, instead of sarcasm, when I point out a logical blunder, I just repeat Robin Williams's *I'm sorry, if you were right, I'd agree with you*. And then to drive the point home, I credit it to the master, Robin Williams. After all, who would dare argue with Robin Williams?" Roberta said.

"Yogi Berra had the best easy way out—*I never said most of the things I said*," Jerry said. Everyone continued to chuckle and giggle over the simple interactions. It was a good relief. Tensions disappeared, at least temporarily, and the group grew even closer. Eric and Connor were now solidly entrenched in the group, and they knew they could realistically die together.

Roberta reviewed the last few weeks. All her fellow survivors had changed, although she didn't like to assign the word "change" to any of them. Change couldn't adequately describe the nuances and details involved. Other than losing some weight and gaining some muscle, only Tom and Ashley had changed physically. Interpersonal relations had changed. Eric and Connor easily fit into that descriptor, and she admitted that she too fit into that box. Rick appeared to have allowed his intellectual curiosity to develop through his otherwise "go along to get along" personality. Paul and Sandy had a momentary lapse in their moral standards, but quickly found their foundation and got themselves back on board. Jerry found his affirmative personality. She wondered how that would affect their future. Sharing some household decisions would be good. Then she wondered why she would welcome a change in that realm. Roberta had enjoyed her family life simply fine. Was it her current vulnerability that welcomed a change, or was she permanently modifying her perspectives? She didn't know, but it was worth considering. Maybe just the fact that she actively considered it was a positive indicator.

Roberta reflected on Tom. He started this adventure three steps down. What kind of inner strength did it take just to pick himself up and move in any direction after burying his parents? Little wonder he couldn't face the campers when he first met them. All he needed was another complication. Tom's true personality emerged when he accepted help; his dedication to the responsibilities he assumed was monumental. It would be a disaster if she didn't have the opportunity to spend a lot more time with Tom.

Eric and Connor's revelations and commitments were significant. They were sincere. They obviously recognized the value of community and that social isolation served no one well. Roberta questioned whether a permanent personality shift was possible in such a short period of time. Personalities didn't shift quickly under normal circumstances, but these weren't normal circumstances. Could the gravity of life in severe conditions trigger significant permanent modifications? Changes in brain processes required rewiring the connections. Is it possible to speed the rewiring by making the new channels primary, and essential through trauma? Those questions were partially answered when she considered how they rescued her. For now it worked for the success of the group.

In any event, fear seemed to have been the consolidating element. Not necessarily fear of dying. It could have been fear of failure, as in Tom's commitment to get everybody out alive. Perhaps the fear of the pain of starvation or freezing. The two most stable individuals were clearly Ben and Ashley. Roberta admired Ashley. Roberta wasn't jealous of Ashley's sexuality; she revered her for recognizing who she was and taking on the world to live it. Beyond that, or perhaps hand in hand with that strength, she was stable, capable, and caring. Ben exuded that same caring strength. Fear didn't seem to affect him. Roberta thought through that and the possible reasons for it. Ben had come a long way from his roots in Alabama. She wondered about the racism fears he must have lived with in the Deep South. Were the fears he faced here in the wilderness no worse than fears he'd lived through? Could he have developed the ability to shed the effects of fear? She wondered. She would like to talk to him about it, but this wasn't the time or place.

As the fire burned down, they fed it and repeated more quotations as they came to mind. One led to another and the campers were happy for that. They didn't want it to end. They put their subconscious thoughts of starvation, freezing, death, and dying aside and enjoyed good company. All good things end, however, and late into the night they banked the fire and settled in for the night.

CHAPTER 17

*D*aylight came late, due to heavy overcast. They felt good that their firewood was safe under the tarp covering their lean-to home. Eric and Connor trudged out of camp with the rifle. They would work hard at hunting. Even if nothing shootable came into their sights, working at it would relieve other thoughts. At one point they took a stand on a small hillock and shared another discussion. There was nothing else to celebrate. The crew maintained the signal fire but didn't bother to waste any smoke-generating materials. Still attempting to avoid depression, Jerry suggested every able body spread out and seek all the firewood they could find. His dark reasoning, that he kept to himself, was that he wanted all the physical work to be finished while their bodies were still fueled. When starvation and fatigue set in, their last gasps could be used to throw sticks on the fire.

Jerry went to the tent to see Tom. Sandy stopped trying to get water on Tom's lips and faced Jerry as he entered. "He's not with it," Sandy whispered.

Late that afternoon, rain followed the overcast. Eric and Connor had returned empty-handed just before dark set in. They ate the last of the caribou jerky and a watery soup made from one potato and one onion. The crew huddled around the fire, mostly in silence until Connor took the floor. "That's a real mountain of firewood we've got started. If we get hungry, we'll be hungry and warm, instead of hungry and cold.

Much better. And by the way, talking of meals, Paul and Sandy, I think we'd all like to thank you for what you've done for us. You made the most from what we had. I wish we'd been able to bring in some more ingredients for you. Eric and I had another little talk today about commitments. We're committed to getting us all out of here. If you think we'd have any chance of going out for help, we'd try it."

"Tom said the cross-country route could swallow a man up with any amount of rain, and that following the riverbank would be next to impossible. That's it. We all thank you for the offer, but our best bet is to stay here and hope we can get some more smoke in the air. Also, the last thing out of Tom's mouth was something that sounded like 'irch lanier . . . gather.' Can anybody make sense out of it?" Jerry asked.

"Anybody seen a birch tree here?" Paul asked.

"Could he have thought we could gather birch limbs big enough to gather and build another boat?" Sandy asked.

"He may have lost track of where we are," Roberta said.

"Okay. We'll keep hunting," Eric said.

Even in the rain with less-than-full stomachs, they felt good about their chances. They'd done everything they could do for themselves and knew they would never give up. If there was a stray caribou or bear or even a rabbit, they would eat it. Commitment.

The rain stopped in the middle of the night and daylight brought only a light overcast. Before light, Eric and Connor set out on another hunt. Jerry decided to start smoke signals. He arranged a tarp so that he could pull it over the fire to entrap the smoke temporarily. By trapping and releasing the smoke alternatively, the smoke would rise in cloud-like puffs. The unnatural appearance of the alternating puffs would be more likely to catch the attention of a bush pilot, he hoped. Everyone was grim. No one complained or criticized anything.

Jerry sent sentinels to high points around the camp to watch for an airplane. After three hours on watch, Rick called out that he saw an airplane on the horizon. Everyone looked for it, and most of the campers also watched it disappear over the horizon. Still not a single outward expression of the disappointment they all felt. Along with the disappointment, each camper individually internalized their belief that they struggled in this together.

"We'll keep smoke in the air for the rest of the day," Jerry said.

Eric and Connor decided to hunt up the river. They thought the cover might be more inviting for game to forage through, so together they spent the morning hours moving through the brush and close to the water on the way up the river. About noon, they decided to change their tactics. Connor suggested that he travel through the brush up to fifty yards away from Eric. That way they could cover more ground, and if he forced game to move away from him, Eric would have a chance to get a shot off. Connor walked away from Eric and they moved as quietly as possible back toward camp. After an hour of stalking almost silently through the brush, Connor noticed something moving through the brush a hundred yards in front of him. He set a course that would more likely move the animal closer to Eric. They now hunted in a more open landscape. Connor continued to close on the last position he had seen movement. His eyes opened wide and he took a deep breath when he saw the first track they had seen since they killed the caribou.

A large fresh bear track etched in the sand. The bear was moving toward Eric. Connor's heart raced as he frantically searched ahead for the bear. He took a step at a time, stepping in the bear's tracks. Twenty yards ahead, Connor could see the tracks before they disappeared into a small gully with low-growing brush. He continued stepping into the bear's tracks. One step. Stop. Look. Listen. Another step. Connor continued until he stood on the edge of the gully, searching ahead for movement or more tracks. Suddenly, the stillness of the wilderness erupted into a ferocious roar as the bear stood erect in the bottom of the gully. Connor jumped back and shouted something unintelligible. The bear growled, and Connor froze. He tried to think. Anything. Ten yards from the bear and he was terrified. Finally, he decided to shout-out for Eric.

"Eric!"

"I'm coming!" Eric ran and stumbled through the low brush, sand, gravel, and dead branches littering the ground. He came around a bush thirty yards from Connor in time to see the bear charge up the gully bank toward Connor. Eric stood erect, put the gun butt to his shoulder, squinted through the telescope, and started to squeeze the trigger. He didn't have much time or room for error. The bear and Eric were in a single embrace. He couldn't wait. He squeezed harder. He felt the recoil, and the muzzle force pushed the barrel up. Eric brought the gun down and watched the bear shudder from a wound somewhere on his upper torso or foreleg. The bear swung around to look at Eric. Connor pushed away from the bear. Before Connor could take another step, the bear whirled back around and batted him to the ground. Eric lifted the rifle bolt and pulled back to eject the empty cartridge. When he pushed the bolt forward to load another cartridge, it wouldn't move forward. Eric frantically worked the mechanism. No success.

As Eric worked the rifle, he watched the bear take a swipe at Connor on the ground. Eric was horrified at the sight and the power of the bear. In a single moment with one swing from a paw full of claws the bear disemboweled Connor. Connor was dead. Eric tried to work the bolt. He couldn't get the next cartridge into the chamber. The thought of options sprinted through his mind. None of them good and no time to consider them. The bear ran toward him. At the last moment he threw the rifle at the bear and began to run. The bear swatted the gun aside and overwhelmed Eric on the ground. Eric noticed blood from a wound on the bears upper foreleg just before the bear ripped his throat open with his fangs. The bear stood and inspected his work. When he was satisfied that Eric could no longer hurt him, he returned to inspect Connor. The bear stood erect and sniffed the air. He surveyed the area and decided to leave before something else could irritate him.

"Did you hear that?" Paul asked.

"Yes. Get a fix on the position. Let's go out to see what they got," Jerry said.

Everyone smiled. Jerry, Rick, and Ben started off in the general direction of the gunshot. They walked briskly through the small bushes and low gullies. After an hour, they stopped and surveyed the area.

"We could get lost out here. Camp is back and just to the right of that small hillock. Let's make sure we know our way back to this point," Jerry said.

"Should we spread out to cover more ground?" Ben asked.

"I think I'd rather we stayed together," Rick said.

"I think Rick might have a good idea," Jerry said. They made specific notes of landmarks and continued the search. They called out for Eric and Connor. Silence answered them.

"I don't like that. Let's carry on together." An hour later they realized they ran a real risk of being away from camp in the dark if they didn't start back.

"What do you think, Jerry?" Ben asked.

"I don't know. I'm worried about them. If we stay out here in the dark, we won't do them or us much good. If they got something, they probably would have cut a piece out and gone back to camp," Jerry said.

"If they're not back at camp, . . . " Rick's voice trailed off to nothing.

"If they're not in camp they're in trouble. I don't think we could do much to find them in the dark. I think we should head back," Ben said.

"I agree. If they're not there, we'll set out again first thing in the morning," Jerry said. They started the miserable walk back to camp. Well after dark, they made it back. No Eric or Connor.

Paul, Sandy, Roberta, and Ashley were anxious about the search and the hunters' status. Jerry told them they didn't find them and that they would go back out in the morning.

"How's Tom?" Jerry asked.

"I've been able to get some water in him, but no other change," Sandy said.

"Anybody see a plane?" Rick asked.

"No," Paul answered.

They sat around the fire and drank warm water. "I'm worried about Connor and Eric. No—scared for them. Why would they fire a shot and not come back?" Paul asked.

"I don't know. I hope we find a good explanation in the morning," Jerry answered.

"Maybe they wounded a caribou and had to chase it down," Sandy said.

"Let's hope that's the case, and let's hope they caught up to it," Roberta added.

Nobody mentioned the other possibility; that they wounded a bear. "Paul, Sandy, Roberta—keep the fires burning, watch for airplanes, and be prepared with bear spray if you need it. Also continue trying to get water into Tom. Ben, Rick, and I will take the pistol and a can of bear spray at first light. We've got to find them." During the dark hours, everybody struggled with the possibilities. None of them slept well because their thoughts always returned to the worst of those possibilities.

At the first hint of light, Ben dressed and rebuilt the fires. Jerry and Rick joined him. "Rick, you carry the pistol. Ben, you take the bear spray. Let's get back to where we left off yesterday." The three men trudged off silently in the mist.

As they approached the spot where they had abandoned the search, they recognized the brush was growing taller and denser. Jerry climbed a small hillock to investigate the landscape then suggested they skirt the dense brush in a direction away from the river.

"Be sure to stay close and pay attention," Rick said.

After another half hour of slow forward progress, Ben noticed a bear's paw print in the gravel. "Look at this," Ben said. They identified more prints and the direction the bear had been moving.

"Oh no." Jerry pointed to a small smatter of blood next to one of the prints.

"This isn't good," Rick said.

"If the bear's moving that way with a wound and there are no boot tracks here, we should backtrack," Ben said.

"Maybe Eric and Connor were chasing the bear from off to the side of the bear's trail. I think we should make a circle here to see if we can pick up their boot tracks," Jerry said. They carefully circled the area around the blood. They found no boot marks. "Okay, it doesn't look like they followed the bear. Let's backtrack." They followed the bear's tracks backward for twenty minutes.

"Awww," Rick turned aside and choked out a few gasps. He would have thrown up, but there was nothing in his stomach. All three men were aghast at the sight. Connor had been ripped apart from the inside. The contents of his abdomen were stretched out on the gravel. On the other side of the gully they found Eric with his throat ripped out and dark blood all around his head and shoulders. The men surveyed the area in complete silence. It didn't take a lot of crime scene investigation to piece together the scenario after they found the jammed rifle. Eric and Connor had wounded the bear and it took vengeance upon them.

"We've got a job to do," Ben said.

"Let's dig out a grave at the bottom of the gully and cover it the best we can," Jerry said. They dug into the sandy gravel a few feet and returned the remains to the earth. They pulled sand and gravel from the gully sides to build a mound over the bodies. Then they broke off willow limbs and stuck them in the ground around the mound to form a fence. That was all they could do. It might help a reconnaissance crew identify the grave. Jerry carried the dysfunctional rifle and, glumly, the men started back to camp. An hour of trudging in silence brought them to another small rise. They decided to take a break with a view. Even with a mainly gray sky, they were able to see the unmistakable smoke signals. At least their signaling mechanism worked. Now, if only some-body would see it. They carried on, tired and disheartened. Hunger was past tense, and it didn't occupy a lot of space.

From the camp hillock, Paul watched a plane disappear over the horizon. When he saw the men approaching, he decided to meet them halfway.

"You've got the rifle. I take that as really bad news."

"They wounded a bear and their gun jammed. The bear killed them both. We buried them the best we could. The bear appears to have run off away from the river," Jerry said.

"That hurts. There's no change in Tom. Sandy got some water in him, but he's still unresponsive."

"We're going to have to give them the bad news. Let's get to camp," Ben said.

Sandy and Ashley were shocked when they heard. Roberta tried to throw up. She was devastated. Her new best friends were gone. For the moment, she thought it was over; she didn't care.

"Let's build our wood supply," Jerry said. Ashley stayed in camp with Tom while the crew went to work.

With the last of the daylight, they sat around the fire and were thankful for warm water. Jerry worked with the rifle. He used his knife to open the magazine cover and removed the four remaining cartridges. He then worked the bolt and discovered that a small pebble blocked the bolt from engaging the next cartridge. Jerry reassembled the rifle and loaded the cartridges in the magazine. When he worked the bolt, the next cartridge properly loaded into the chamber. Jerry repeated the process twice more until he was satisfied the gun worked correctly. Then he removed the live cartridges and continued to work the moving parts. He found the craftsmanship precise and the tactile feel of a finely engineered tool pleasing. He thought maybe it was no accident that gun owners liked to hold and operate their guns. He thought maybe demanding that they be allowed to carry them into bars and schools was a bit too much like a baby and his favorite pacifying blanket, though. He reminisced about handling some of the tools his company manufactured and how he enjoyed inspecting them and operating the mechanisms.

"That's a damn shame. A stupid little pebble killed them."

"And maybe us," Sandy said.

"That gun was their pride and joy. They knew how to use and take care of it. It must have gone bad when we lost the boat. It was loose on the gravel," Rick said.

"I wonder if Eric and Connor might have had a good idea about trying to walk out," Roberta said.

"The last clear thing Tom told me was that going down the river could be treacherous and that the land between here and Fort Yukon would be impossible if it rained hard," Jerry said.

"It wasn't bad out there today," Rick said.

"Things can change quickly, as we've seen," Ben said.

"Let's sleep on it," Paul said.

Now, even to Jerry, the sight of the bear's vengeance, plus hunger and disappearing planes, made the thought of hiking out less impossible. Tom wasn't available to reinforce the obvious.

Roberta went to bed, but she didn't sleep for an hour or two. The logic was simple. She tried to put the facts on the table. If they waited too long before they attempted to walk out, they wouldn't have the strength to walk out. She estimated that option was closing fast. If they left at any time and the weather changed, they would probably die. If they stayed at the camp and no plane came, they would definitely die. Therefore, if they were going to leave, they had to leave soon. She guessed that five people would try to make it to Fort Yukon. The odds of survival didn't change much, whether two or five tried. Tom and Ashley wouldn't be able to travel, and someone would stay with them.

She estimated the chance of a severe weather change at 30 percent, in which case all the trekkers would die. If the weather didn't change, she estimated the chance of making it to Fort Yukon would be 75 percent. She estimated the chance of a plane coming at 50 percent. If a plane came and the weather didn't change, the chance of finding the trekkers would be 60 percent, she guessed. If a plane didn't come, but they made it to Fort Yukon, the chance of rescuing the people at the camp would be 100 percent. Then she tried to put it all together. This type of mental gymnastics was something Roberta had mastered. She disregarded the possibility that hunger, depression, and desperation could cloud her calculation considerations or presumed probabilities.

If they all stayed at the camp there was a 50 percent chance of survival for all of them. The odds of the trekkers' survival equated to 70 percent surviving the weather. And if that happened, there was a 75 percent chance of them making it to Fort Yukon. Therefore, 70 percent times 75 percent yielded 52.5 percent; 50 percent was close enough. There was a slightly better than 50 percent chance that all of them would survive. So far so good, she thought. That minimal positive difference wouldn't make it worth the 30 percent risk of certain death for the trekkers. She decided to attempt the calculation that would yield the incremental value of taking the risk.

If a plane came and the weather didn't change, there was a 60 percent chance a search would find the trekkers if they otherwise didn't make it out. Therefore, 70 percent (weather doesn't kill them) times 60 percent (chance a search plane would find them) times 25 percent (chance they would not have made it out, even without bad weather) yielded 10.5 percent. That equation said that 10.5 percent was the incremental value in making an unsuccessful attempt to walk out. She added that amount to her first number, the 52.5 percent she got by the trekkers not being killed by the weather and making it to Fort Yukon, so, 52.5 percent plus 10.5 percent yielded 63 percent. That meant, if they left, the survival value number was 63 percent. If they stayed, the probability was 50 percent. Given her assumptions about probabilities, it was better to try to get to Fort Yukon, if the weather didn't change. Even if the weather changed, there was still a chance that a plane would come and find them before they died. Roberta didn't try to calculate those probabilities. She simply added a plus sign to her 63 percent.

She posited the results in memory and reconsidered the variables. If they all stayed, there was a 50 percent chance of everybody surviving. If five people left for Fort Yukon, there was a 63 plus percent chance of everyone surviving and a 30 percent certainty of five people dying. If five people died, there was still a 50 percent chance of the three people at the camp surviving. But, if only two people tried to make it to Fort Yukon, there was still a 30 percent certainty of them dying, but a 50 percent chance of six people at the camp surviving. It made sense that more people should want to stay at camp. Roberta knew she should assign a range of probabilities for each of the variables as she had explained around the fire up the river. Then she should do the multiple calculations for each iteration. Her concentration failed her. She worried that her calculations were incomplete and therefore less reliable. She gave up when she realized that her concentration was failing her.

But, but, but, what if the probability of a weather change were reversed. Roberta knew the statistical manipulations required to calculate the values for sure death for some versus the possible rescue of others. She didn't attempt it because she didn't want to play god with real lives, her friends' lives. Who dies, who survives was not a question she could deal with.

If the chance of a weather change were 70 percent, instead of 30 percent, the probabilities changed significantly for the worse. She tried to play weather person for Interior Alaska, but soon gave it up. She went to sleep thinking she at least tried to put the question into perspective.

Sandy went to sleep knowing they had a few days without food before true desperation set in. Paul wrestled with the knowledge that whatever happened, he would face it with dignity. Ben confronted the death of his partner by reliving the sight of Eric and Connor. His great-est fear was that he would have to try to console Walt's wife. Annie would help him, but the experience would be devastating. Rick tried to sleep, but all he could manage was to worry. He couldn't concentrate on anything specific. There was so much happening—choices, hunger, what would the group decide. He just wanted something positive he could follow. Jerry contemplated the discussion regarding trekking across to Fort Yukon. He trusted Tom but wondered about the weather. He fell asleep and slept well.

A bright, clear sky ushered in a brand-new day. Jerry stirred the fires, then climbed the camp hillock to search the area, not only for aircraft, but also for a wounded bear. He found neither. He took a cup of water to Tom and tried to get him to sip even a taste. He thought Tom got some into his mouth. He tried to moisten Tom's lips, hoping he was doing the right thing. Paul put a pot of water on the grill and asked Jerry how Tom looked.

Ben walked to the riverbank and stared down toward where the river would have carried his partner. Then he climbed up the hillock and stared out to where they buried Eric and Connor. Maybe I'll be next, he thought. In the meantime, he was with the crew and would work on anything that would help. The satisfaction Jerry gained by having a mountainous pile of firewood available wasn't enough to bring a smile to his face.

Ashley was fragile, but completely cognizant. She wished she were physically able to join in to help with any chores or trekking require-ments. Unfortunately, there was too little to do. Paul and Sandy's pri-mary responsibility had been reduced to boiling water. Rick walked around, trying to fit into the activities. He fit in perfectly. He was their best worrier.

Paul took more water into the tent for Tom. He had minimal suc-cess in getting the water into Tom's mouth. When Paul exited the tent, he joined the crew standing around the fire, sipping warm water. "In Roberta's terms, let's talk about options," Paul said.

"I figure we've got a couple of days before things get really serious, desperation serious," Sandy said.

"Maybe we should consider doubling our chances," Paul said.

"How do we double our chances?" Rick asked eagerly.

"Put our eggs in two baskets," Jerry said, neglecting to remind himself, or anybody, about Tom's advice. For whatever reason, the security of the camp held little interest.

Without adequate knowledge of weather, probabilities, or hiking conditions, Rick liked the idea of doubling their chances.

"I tried to calculate some probabilities last night," Roberta said.

"And?" Paul asked.

"It's not good," Roberta answered.

"Worse than staying here?" Paul shot back before Roberta could continue.

"It depends on probabilities. I don't have enough information to put everybody's life on the line with incomplete data," Roberta said.

"What assumptions did you use?" Ben asked.

"I assumed that at least two of us would try to walk to Fort Yukon. I don't think one of us should try it alone. I don't know if two, three, four, or five would increase the chances of getting to Fort Yukon. I know that the people who don't try to get to Fort Yukon aren't at risk of certain death if the weather changes." She didn't get distracted with the fact that she couldn't consider all the numbers in her head. If she had her computer, she would have run the calculations for all the probabilities.

Again, Paul interrupted and asked, "How far away do we think Fort Yukon is?"

"I think it's about fifty miles," Jerry said.

"Is that possible?" Rick asked.

"Tom thought it might be possible, but only in good weather," Jerry said.

"And that's the assumption I can't know how to make. If we assume that there's a 70 percent chance the weather won't change, there's a slightly better incremental chance of all of us getting out alive. But, if there's a 30 percent chance the weather won't change, the probability is very bad. Certain death for those that go and no change for those that stay. I can't take responsibility for the weather," Roberta said.

"Wait a minute. If the weather doesn't change, isn't it almost certain that everybody lives?" Rick asked.

"Not quite certain, but basically that's right. But if the weather changes, it's certain death out there."

Rick shifted from his usual indecisive attitude to a positive statement of his desires. "I want to try to make it out to Fort Yukon."

"Do you understand that we don't know what the weather will do? And, is hunger and depression clouding your judgment?"

"I understand that. I'll take the chance."

"I'm not saying you're wrong, if you've considered the consequences," Jerry said. "Ashley, you've been in tough situations. What are you thinking?" he asked.

"I'm in no condition to walk out. I'll stay here and care for Tom."

"I understand that, but I trust your judgment. What do you think about the chances of walking out?"

"First of all, I won't be going, so I can't guess at the chances for you. It's just a guess at this point."

"Ben, where are you?" Jerry asked.

"Well, I'm not going to leave Ashley alone with Tom. Rick going by himself is not a good idea. All of you must make the decision for yourselves with no recriminations. If anybody survives, never question anybody else's decision. On the positive side, there could be a meal out there. We know there's a bear out there somewhere. Nobody knows the probabilities of a plane or the weather. I think Roberta's assumptions are as good as we can get; none of us know. On the negative side, if the weather changes, everybody out there will die. Back on the positive side, if you make it to Fort Yukon, we all live. If we all stay here, who knows? Everybody must pick an option individually."

"Ben's right. Whatever decisions we make, there will be no blame or criticism," Jerry said.

"If you all go, it's okay with me. The wood is here and I'm perfectly capable of getting water to Tom and throwing sticks on the fire. I've spent a lot of time in the high desert alone," Ashley said.

"It seems to me there's a chance of killing something out there. If we do, we all live," Paul said.

"We would have to travel light and fast," Jerry said. There seemed to be a growing wave of optimism for the chance of making it to Fort Yukon.

"Probably just a sleeping bag, knife, matches, maybe tents. If it rains, we die anyway," Sandy said.

"Another positive twist is that if we kill something the first day, we could haul it back here and postpone the trek with full bellies. I think we should go, try it," Roberta said.

"Who wants to walk out?" Jerry asked. Everybody except Ben raised a hand.

"Take the rifle, we'll keep the pistol here. You better move out as soon as you can get packed. If a plane comes here, we'll search the route for you. Stay together and good luck," Ben said.

Jerry made an inventory of packs and supplies and made one last check of Ben and Ashley. Jerry gave Ashley a light hug, shook Ben's hand, and led the trekkers toward the last sighting of an airplane.

CHAPTER 18

"Find anything?"

"No. I flew every inch of both sides of the Yukon all the way from Fort Yukon to the landing zone below the Porcupine," Dave replied.

"I can't go back up there for a few days. I've got a group to pick up off the glacier near Seward. I'm leaving in the morning," John said.

"Yeah, and I've got that shuttle job over at Yakutat. I'm going to be gone for almost a week. It's not like Jim to miss a pickup date. If there were ice on the river, we could find them anywhere up the Porcupine River or even further up. There's no sign of ice. If I had time, I'd fly up to the starting point and come back down the entire river system." Dave shook his head, wondering why Jim's group weren't where they were supposed to be. Either Jim and the canoes were camped out safely on the lower reaches of the river system above the confluence of the Porcupine and the Yukon or they were in serious trouble, victims of the earthquake. He thought he would call Candy and ask her to fly up to the starting point of Jim's trip and follow the route all the way down. She would be back in a day or two.

Dave went to the cabinet and pulled out the trip details Jim had given him. He confirmed that, without ice on the river, they were due at the haul-out site on the Yukon, downriver from the confluence of the Porcupine, two days ago. Jim had never missed a scheduled date; he took great pride in that. There was no reason for them to be on the

Porcupine. Once they reached that river, it was a simple ride to the Yukon. Dave scrawled a note and left it on his desk in the flying service office he owned with John. He walked to the window and looked out at the overcast sky at the end of their runway.

"Let's call Johnson and see if he can help us find them. He knows that country better than anybody," John said.

"Yeah, do it."

John dialed the number he had for Johnson. No answer. Twenty minutes later he tried again. Still no answer. John decided to call a mutual friend. Fred said he hadn't seen him for a couple of weeks. He thought he might be in Juneau. He also said he had been wanting to go down to Seattle for a while. John and Dave walked to the hangar for a final inspection of their airplanes before they left for an important rendezvous with vulnerable people waiting. When they were satisfied, John drove home to dinner. John's wife, Zoe, would manage the flying service office while the fliers were gone. John told Zoe to find Jim's file and verify the starting point, then call Candy, the young pilot he had hired. He told Zoe it was important that she contact Candy and get her to start a reconnaissance on the river system. Zoe said she would do it.

In the morning, Dave flew off to Yakutat to perform the shuttle service they had contracted. John left shortly thereafter on his way to Seward. He flew over the glacier in the afternoon, recognized his campers, and dropped a small parachute supporting a box packed with a special meal for their last night on the glacier. John flew back to Seward and waited for the next day's afternoon pickup. As planned and after a good night's sleep, he fueled up, did his inspection, and flew to the glacier. Glaciers always demanded attention. He would prefer a landing on a gravel riverbank any day. Ice on the glaciers shifted, cracked, and melted. It was unstable and not predictable. John flew over the glacier and found his company waving enthusiastically. He circled twice, trying to recognize any dangerous ice. He didn't find a problem and made a nice safe landing in the company's six-passenger airplane.

His campers took pride in their care for the wilderness. They had their equipment packaged, and garbage was neatly packed in a designated duffle. It was a good group. John packed the plane and positioned the five campers for weight distribution, then he started to taxi. An uneventful takeoff and flight to Juneau satisfied everybody. John spent most of the flight worrying about Jim's crew. John knew Jim personally; he also knew Branch's reputation. It would take serious trouble to put the people in his care in a desperation mode. He knew the wilderness, bears, and bad-weather camping.

An incident came to mind that made John confident that the campers would survive. Branch had accepted a challenge with substantial monetary reward. The challenge was for Branch to be dropped in the wilderness wearing only a pair of jeans and a sweatshirt, barefoot, and with no tools. He would win the challenge, along with the money, if he survived for two weeks. After two weeks, a plane landed with a doctor to retrieve him. Branch welcomed them to his camp wearing a leather shirt and moccasins. He offered them caribou jerky and smoked salmon. That cemented Branch's reputation in Alaska.

As John analyzed the situation with Jim's expedition, he realized belatedly that if something had gone wrong, they could easily be on the Porcupine riverbank. Just before dark and after receiving a healthy tip, John tied his plane down and went to a hotel, awaiting his flight home in the morning. He called Zoe and asked about Candy. Zoe told him the shocking news.

As asked, Zoe had contacted Candy and relayed John's concerns. Candy had then flown down Jim's route until she found Johnson's airplane in the middle of the river. Candy landed on the riverbank, verified the wing numbers, and inspected the equipment on the riverbank. She flew to Fairbanks to complete a report for the FAA. She would be back at the office early in the morning. That information added a new twist to missing people on the river. He wondered if somehow Johnson's plight, or the fate of his clients, was entwined with Jim and his missing crew.

John instructed Zoe to have Candy fuel the two-seater she was fly-ing and have it ready for him. He would refuel the larger plane with much greater capacity and range and have her take it out to follow the remainder of Jim's route all the way back. John would fly the two-seater up the Porcupine. Logic told him there were even more people missing on the river system. Given that, John checked out of the hotel and made a night flight home.

CHAPTER 19

Conditions remained unchanged for miles away from the campsite. Relatively flat ground, low-growing willows, brush, and occasional gullies stretched out before them. Jerry took every opportunity to climb to high ground to set landmarks, search for game, and even look back to Ashley, Ben, and Tom. The sky remained clear, not a cloud on the horizon. That reaffirmed Jerry's decision to accompany the trekkers. He looked back one more time. The gray smoke with occasional puffs spiraled high into the sky. He was encouraged.

At midafternoon Jerry, Roberta, Paul, Sandy, and Rick continued to make good time across the damp ground. No standing water interrupted their progress. The clear sky gave them hope. They marched single file with little talk. They wasted no energy.

"Without the need to stop for meals, we make pretty good time," Sandy said.

"I'd stop if there were a reason, but let's keep after it," Rick said.

Jerry climbed another small rise to scout the area. He had almost expected to find a hoof- or bear-claw print on the trail. He scanned the bushes for movement. Still and silent. He looked back and squinted, trying to find the smoke signal. There it was, slightly offline from where he expected to find it. Finding it made him feel better. He walked off the mound and continued to lead his crew.

An hour and a half later, they approached standing water. It appeared too deep to wade through. The opposite shore was dry fifty yards away. Jerry scanned the immediate area for a high spot from which he could find a trail around the water. He found the high spot and climbed up. He used the telescope on the rifle to survey the area. The water extended to the left as far as he could see. To the right, it appeared that the water extended about a half mile. Jerry considered testing the water depth for a try at wading across, or just biting the bullet and walking around it. He decided that remaining relatively dry at this time, late in the afternoon, would be safer, and he directed the crew to follow him around the water. From his vantage point on the mound he didn't recognize more serious water ahead, but the thought that serious bogs could lay in wait concerned him. The trip around the pool presented only a minor distraction. They rounded the wet obstruction and found themselves on safe sand and gravel, again moving toward Fort Yukon. The sun dropped below the horizon but left enough light to allow walking slowly for another half hour.

When it was too dark to take a safe step, Jerry declared they were through for the day. The crew pulled sleeping bags out and crawled in.

"How do you feel about our progress today?" Paul asked.

"I think we crossed as much ground as we could have asked for. Two more days and I think we're home."

"We can do this," Sandy said.

"We're going to do this," Roberta reassured everyone.

That was the conversation for the night. All the trekkers knew they had done everything they could have done. They considered it their obligation to get to Fort Yukon and send rescue to Ashley, Ben, and Tom. The air remained still and cool. Everybody slept well.

Jerry woke with the faintest hint of light creeping in over the horizon. He crawled out and didn't find it necessary to pronounce it a good morning or issue any other inducements to jump up and get on the trail; the others were also already getting up. The sky was clear, the air was cold, and the ground was relatively firm. A few mouthfuls of water and they were off. An hour after the sun made an appearance, Jerry climbed another small rise and looked back for the smoke signals. He worried that he didn't immediately recognize anything in the sky except a few clouds on the horizon. He squinted through the scope on the rifle. At last, he identified the thin wisp of faint color in the sky. There was no way the signal would ever be recognized as anything other than natural if Jerry didn't know better. In other circumstances, the trekkers would have considered it boring. Brush, sand, gravel, small gullies, and minor water hazards extended before them as far as they could see and presented no threats or interests to their journey to safety.

With the only concern being to put one foot in front of the other, Roberta resumed her struggle with apparent hypocrisy. She thought that before she could deal with specific arguments, she should reestablish who she was, what she believed, and how that fit the foundation she believed in. Whenever she found reason to touch the earth to find firm footing for an argument, she usually started with René Descartes. Two of his quotes came immediately to mind: one, "Divide each difficulty into as many parts as is feasible and necessary to resolve it," and two, "Cogito ergo sum"—I think, therefore I am. That quote by itself wasn't as important to Roberta now as much as Descartes' lifelong search to divine it. Descartes was obsessed with the desire to find one absolute truth. A truth that could stand the test of time. A thought that would be irrefutable.

Roberta always assumed that her basic arguments were solid—perhaps not as irrefutable as the Latin, but good. To rebuild her foundation, Roberta began stripping off the fallacies. Okay, she thought, I must admit Christmas and all it spawned is a hoax. She didn't find it necessary to condemn all religion. Most religions preached good things and provided some invaluable services. Why must the most popular religions be based in myths, great lies? The immaculate conception, a great anathema to science, to natural law itself. She had participated in promoting the myth. She knew she couldn't claim ignorance; she knew better. She would have to admit hypocrisy. Her best defense might be to admit that she failed to analyze the facts. This wasn't fun. When she returned to Seattle, there were people that would delight in adding to her misery. She would have to think about how to write about it. Roberta knew one thing: she had to do it.

Rick began to think. He followed the footprints in front of him, but he wasn't paying attention to the trail or the landscape, not even hunger. He concentrated on the philosophical fireside chats of which he had contributed little more than elementary questions. Now the fog of innocence began to dissipate. He first considered the harsh denunciation of Christmas, and the irreconcilable argument between belief and science. He appreciated the statement that gave him the ability to declare, that he wanted to believe, without fear of any condemnation. He churned the arguments for science and belief in his mind and concluded that if he had to choose a side, he had missed the point of the entire discussion. The philosophy at hand dictated that logic and science were pure and that nobody should be so ignorant as to argue against the scientific method. But, equally important, on yet another plane, personal beliefs were legitimate. Nobody should ever question what somebody believed without provocation. The arguments for science and logic are solid and the topic of Christmas was the natural culmination of previously discussed airtight arguments; rebuking lies, hypocrisy, white privilege, and racism.

For the next mile, Rick recirculated his reconciliation thoughts weighing them with specific statements his fellow campers had made. He thought he had begun to build a foundation that he could stand firm upon in discussions around another fire someday. He focused on a statement Sandy made. She found it offensive when religious people attempted to push their religion on her. Rick thought, yes, that was offensive, probably to most believers. Why do people find it necessary to project their beliefs onto others? Was it domination or insecurity?

Power in numbers. The greater our numbers, the more power we have. But power over what? If your religion is personal to you, you have total control over it, he thought. Rick concluded his self-questioning by realizing that if he lived a good life with honor and respect, he wouldn't have to sell his beliefs to anybody.

Just before midday, a light breeze blew against their backs. It was pleasing. As they pressed on, however, the wind grew stronger. Jerry found another view area. He scanned the area ahead of them and saw nothing but more of the same. He looked back. Now he became concerned. The low clouds on the horizon behind them earlier had grown larger, darker, and uglier. He climbed off the hill and consulted his charges. "We made a decision and we're going to have to live with it. The clouds are building behind us. I'm afraid we're in a race for our lives."

"We can't waste any time," Roberta said.

They started again at a stiff pace. They bypassed a small pond approximately an acre in size. No animal tracks. They maintained a steady pace as the wind blew in gusts. The sky grew darker and their spirits churned with the sky. The sun no longer presented an object in the sky, and only a portion of the sky was a bit lighter than the rest.

"Here it comes," Rick said.

"Yeah, I feel the drops too," Sandy said.

Jerry tried to imagine that he could find some elevated land if the rain accumulated and flooded the low-lying area. Until they needed it, they pursued a course to Fort Yukon. Jerry recognized the undulating terrain in the area in front of them and thought they would continue until there was only just enough light to give them time to set up two tents on the highest landing available. Finally, the day ended. Almost dark, two tents erected, and a steady rain. Trekkers zipped the tents closed and fumbled to unpack their sleeping bags. Like the previous night, there was little conversation. Unlike the previous night, they feared what conditions they would face all too soon.

At the Porcupine campsite, Ashley assumed responsibility for efforts to hydrate Tom. A few drops at a time and moisture on his lips; it wasn't enough. It continued to concern her. She decided to place a damp towel on Tom's forehead, a treatment she had appreciated when she was stuck in bed after a cow had attacked her, rolled her over, and ripped a nasty gash on her lower back with a foot-long horn. Ben gathered more firewood, stacked it neatly, and fed the fires.

"That sky doesn't look good. I fear for them," Ben said.

"I hope those clouds are a false alarm."

"I'm not going to try to make smoke until the sky lightens up a little. Nobody would see it."

Ben and Ashley watched the weather change. It wasn't good. The wind gusted in strong bursts, and the dark and dangerous-looking clouds blew over the landscape. Just before dark, Ben went to the signal fire and banked it to assure that he would have coals in the morning. Ashley attempted to get more water into Tom. Then they curled themselves in their sleeping bags under the protective tarp and watched the fire. The rains came, hard rain. They feared for their friends. They knew the trekkers were in serious trouble.

"Right now, I wish they hadn't gone," Ashley said.

"Hindsight's always better. At the time, they thought it was a fifty-fifty proposition. I wish Tom would snap out of it. After all he did for us, all your good work after we found him on the trail, it all seems wasted. Jerry told me his last words, but we couldn't figure them out."

"What was it again?"

"Something like 'irch lanier . . . gather.'"

"Doesn't make sense. Was he saying to stay together for some reason?"

"Right now, it seems like that made a lot of sense."

"For his age, he seems so mature, wise, and capable. I'd like to know him after he has a chance to spend some time at a university," Ashley said.

"You're right. I believe he's a man that could accomplish anything he set his mind to. I'd like to have known his parents. That wisdom didn't just happen."

"It seemed like Jerry and Roberta were ready to adopt him and give him a chance in Seattle."

"We can only hope that can still happen," Ben said.

The wind gusted and rattled the nylon walls of the lean-to. The driven rain continued to saturate the ground. The direction of the wind shifted by almost a hundred eighty degrees. "That shift in the wind direction might be telling us that the low-pressure area is moving by us," Ashley said. "Maybe this could be a short-term storm. When I was on the ranch, I could read the weather well, but here, there are factors to consider that I just don't understand. Back on the high desert, it almost always got cold after a big storm. I hope that's not too severe here. If our friends get wet, the cold could be devastating.

They took a chance, and maybe by taking that chance, they gave us a chance. I wish we were together again. There's nothing we can do for them. I can't think of anything else we can do for Tom, either."

"Poor Eric and Connor. I've never seen an attitude shift like that. They went from completely obtuse, aloof, and—quite frankly—disgusting, to a position of ultimate commitment to the group. That was a rewarding experience. It seemed like they'd never been forced to face reality. It's a shame it came in such severe circumstances. I believe they had a lot to offer. Now it's our burden to carry their gifts forward. I'll commit to that," Ben said.

"That's a comforting thought. I'll carry that along with you.

I want to get sick all over again when I think of Walt. He died in a noble cause, but it wasn't right. He was sensible and good-willed. He jumped right in to help with Tom's wounds."

"He was more than my partner. He was a truly good and loyal friend. I can't imagine how I'm going to tell Joan. He fought racism. Not a passive dislike; he took true action-oriented positions. I used to have to tell him to calm down, slow down, they have to live with their hate."

"That's interesting. You're right. Haters must live with it and it keeps them from moving forward. When you spend your life hating, you miss out."

"I believe that. It hurts, and I try to protect my kids from it, but they still see it."

"That kind of hate is something I haven't missed on this trip."

"Hard price to pay. I'm going to try to sleep. I'll see you in the morning."

The wind and rain accompanied sleep. Rain came faster than the ground could swallow it. Puddles grew into pools and rivulets connected pools to form larger pools. In the hours prior to daylight, the intensity decreased, and the temperature dropped. When Ben rolled over at daylight the rain had stopped, but ice had formed on the edges of the water pools. Daylight didn't bring warmer air. The temperature continued to drop.

Ashley went to Tom. She moistened his lips and managed to get him to swallow a small amount of water. That was an improvement. Ben refueled the campfire, then went to the signal fire and fed it enough wood to get a good blaze. When it all ignited, they had a strong signal fire at the ready. Thanks to good planning, they had plenty of combustible materials.

"I got some water into Tom. He didn't try to talk, but he swallowed the water."

"That's a good sign. Let's hope our friends out there are making progress too."

"I'm going to try to climb that little hill. I want to see what they're up against."

"Do you want some help?"

"No, let me try it." Ashley walked toward the little hill and carefully put one foot in front of the other with the aid of a small stick until she stood on top. She looked out over the stark landscape. Pooling water clearly invaded most of the area. If it weren't for their predicament, she would have considered it a worthy photographic study. She turned and faced the river. Upstream, where they came from, downstream, where their boat should have taken them; no guarantees out here, she thought. She was thankful Ben stayed at the camp with her; at least she would have a companion to the end. Crying wouldn't do any good, and she set that emotion aside. Besides, she wanted to be strong for Ben. He was in the same situation.

Ashley sat on the hilltop and looked over the camp. She watched Ben go to the signal fire and build it up. He sat next to that fire until the new wood blazed, then he piled on the green material and watched the smoke spiral into the cold air. When the green material generated enough smoke, Ben pulled the tarp over the fire to capture the smoke. When it filled the tarp, Ben pulled the tarp back and released a large cloud. She watched Ben repeat the process several times until a column of smoke puffs sailed high over the camp. She remembered how she had built smoke-signal fires on the high desert just for fun. Oh well, it was fun once. Ben quit creating the puffs and Ashley climbed off the hill to join him at the campfire. She could feel her own weakness. Starvation was taking a toll. She also recognized that Ben moved slowly, and his face told the secret of his condition. It was time to hydrate Tom.

Late in the afternoon, Ben climbed the hill and scanned the horizon all around. He noted that the water had not dissipated. Although the day had been dry, the water pools dominated the landscape. The water accumulation resulted from the runoff of a much larger source, he assumed. He stumbled off the hill and made his way to the signal fire. He banked that fire and returned to Ashley at the campfire. He was thankful that Jerry had insisted on building a huge pile of firewood.

"The water level hasn't changed all day. That's not good news," Ben said.

"Ben, oh excuse me, but I can see in your face that this starvation is taking a toll. And I can feel it too. Our friends out there worked hard for two days, and who knows what they faced today. I'm scared for them."

"I don't see how they could move through a landscape like what we can see."

"Let's hope something changes in the morning."

The night air cleared and sent a freezing chill over the area. Ice covered all the ponds, and Ashley's exhaled words carried a visible reminder of the temperature. "Let me help you get the smoke signals in the air."

"Don't take a chance on puncturing a lung. I can do it." Ben's legs felt creaky and he couldn't find the strength he thought should be in there somewhere. He struggled to the signal fire and flung a lot of wood on the banked fire. "I'll go back and make signal clouds when it gets hot enough."

"Tom sipped just a little water. It's so cold, I didn't put the towel on his forehead."

"If he comes to, he'd just suffer with us. I don't know what to think, other than hoping for a plane to get him real medical help."

"We're not giving up."

When the flames in the signal fire blazed, Ben walked slowly to his pile of green material and threw it on. The smoke accumulated, and he used the tarp to produce smoke-puff signals. Periodically, he returned to the signal fire and repeated the process.

Early in the afternoon, Ashley exited Tom's tent and watched Ben work the tarp. Again she reminisced; I've done that. There's nothing new in the world, just the circumstances.

"Ben, Ben." Ashley shouted in her loudest voice, but it came out in little more than a loud whisper. Ben didn't hear her. The rattle of the tarp made too much interference. Ashley raised one arm and waved. Finally, Ben noticed. He dropped the tarp and stared back as if to ask what she wanted. Ashley pointed in the direction of the engine sound she thought she heard. Ben looked down the river. He didn't see any-thing. Then he heard the sound too. Ben moved back to the signal fire at a fast stumble, grabbed the tarp, and accumulated more smoke. He released the smoke and watched a large puff climb into the clear sky. He repositioned the tarp and waited for more smoke to accumulate.

"There it is!" he shouted. He released the smoke and scrambled back to Ashley. They stood together on the bank and watched the plane grow larger.

"Now, I'm going to need some help. Ashley, will you please help me explain this to Walt's wife?"

"Of course I will."

At last, John used his right foot on the pedal to move the rudder slightly and that turned the plane toward the two people standing on the bank, waving their arms. He flew directly over them. A mile later he turned and flew back over the gravel riverbank, inspecting it for a possible landing. The pilot made one more pass and brought his small two-seat plane down for a landing.

Ben and Ashley made their way to the plane slowly. John recognized two very weak, emaciated people. He jumped out of his plane and ran toward them. "Are you with Jim's Canoe Trips?"

"Yes!" Ashley cried.

"What's left of it."

"You're late. We've been searching the river closer to where you belong."

"Oh no! We should have known. Have we been out here that long? They should never have tried to walk out," Ben whispered.

Horror etched Ashley's face. The one fact that everybody should have considered was completely disregarded. Everybody, at one time, knew a plane would come. She cursed the knowledge—"'irch lanier . . . gather.' sEARCH pLANE NEAR– stay toGETHER. We should have known. Options are worthless if they're not armed with all the facts."

"What're you talking about?" John asked.

"Five people decided to try to walk to Fort Yukon for help."

"From here?"

"Yes, four days ago."

"Oh no."

"We've got a man that needs medical in the tent over there. Can you fly him out?"

"Let's have a look." The pilot followed Ashley and Ben to the tent. The pilot crawled in and leaned over Tom. He put his fingers on his throat. Then he placed his ear over Tom's mouth and nose. He shook his head and crawled out of the tent. "This man's dead."

"Ahhh!" Ashley wailed. "I just gave him water a half hour ago."

"I'm sorry. I'm an EMT and he's dead."

"Can you organize a search for our friends out there?"

"I will, but did they have food and equipment?"

"No food. A gun, two tents, and sleeping bags."

"We'll try to find them. That's miserable territory right now with all the ice and water. Let's get one of you in the plane. Then I'll call for another search plane between here and Fort Yukon, and I'll come back."

"Be careful with her. She's got a couple of broken ribs."

The pilot helped Ashley into the seat, closed the door, and went around the plane to his seat. He clicked his radio to life.

Through the open window, Ashley whispered, "Our wilderness spa."

Ben smiled wryly.

CPSIA information can be obtained
at www.ICGtesting.com
Printed in the USA
BVHW070812160621
609629BV00007B/614